"Tell me that desire isn't crawling along your veins at this moment."

He whispered to her in a low, wickedly seductive voice. "Tell me that you don't want me to kiss you, caress you, make love to you now...here in this room...on this floor...in front of this fire. Tell me that you don't want me, Judith. Tell me...."

MIRANDA LEE is Australian, living near Sydney. Born and raised in the bush, she was boarding-school educated, and briefly pursued a classical music career before moving to Sydney and embracing the world of computers. Happily married, with three daughters, she began writing when family commitments kept her at home. She likes to create stories that are believable, modern, fast paced and sexy. Her interests include reading meaty sagas, doing word puzzles, gambling and going to the movies.

Books by Miranda Lee

HARLEQUIN PRESENTS

MIRANDA LEE

Night of Shame

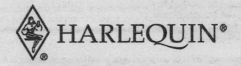

TORONTO • NEW YORK • LONDON
AMSTERDAM • PARIS • SYDNEY • HAMBURG
STOCKHOLM • ATHENS • TOKYO • MILAN • MADRID
PRAGUE • WARSAW • BUDAPEST • AUCKLAND

ISBN 0-373-11990-9

NIGHT OF SHAME

First North American Publication 1998.

CHAPTER ONE

I CAN'T possibly face him, Judith agonised, her eyes squeezing shut against the thought of seeing him again. Seven years might have passed, but she had never forgotten or forgiven, either herself or the perpetrator of her shame and guilt.

'What ever possessed you to invite him?' she cried, green eyes flying open. 'Tonight is a pre-wedding party, not a business get-together.'

The tall man standing by the mantelpiece continued calmly smoking his pipe, one hand resting on the marble shelf.

'Did you hear me, Raymond?' Judith said sharply. 'I asked you why you invited Alexander Fairchild.'

Raymond sighed patiently then sat down in his usual armchair beside the fireplace. Leaning forward, he slowly stoked the burning logs. Sparks shot up into the chimney. He didn't look at her, just stared into the glowing embers.

'Why shouldn't I have invited him?' he said at last in an irritatingly calm voice.

'Because you hardly know him, for one thing! You only met at lunchtime.'

He looked up then, and shrugged. 'What has that got to do with anything? Besides, how was I to know it would cause trouble? I had no idea you even knew the man.'

Judith wanted to scream. How could he sit there, treating her panic so casually? Couldn't he see she was in danger of falling apart?

Judith strode towards his chair, her fists clenching and unclenching at her sides. 'Uninvite him, Raymond,' she said in a low, desperate voice. 'Please. I beg of you.'

'You still haven't explained what you've got against the man. Or where and when you met.'

'He's a bastard,' Judith stated agitatedly. 'A rotten bastard!'

One of Raymond's eyebrows shot up. 'It's not like you to swear, my dear. Now why, pray tell, do you call him such names? He seemed a decent chap to me.'

'You don't know the man. *I* do. And I really do not wish to discuss him. You'll just have to take my word for it.'

She spun away, face flushed, heart racing.

My God, I'll have to stop this, she thought frantically. Or crack up completely. I must pull myself together. It's the shock, that's all. Suddenly hearing his name after all these years, and, worse, the prospect of actually seeing him again.

The thought of spending even one moment in his company was too much to contemplate, let alone a whole evening.

'I can't uninvite him,' Raymond stated matter-of-factly. 'I don't know what hotel he's staying at.'

Judith whirled back to face her fiancé. 'Then I

simply can't go. I won't be in the same room as that man, I tell you.'

Judith knew immediately she'd taken the wrong tack with Raymond over this issue. When his face hardened, she sank down in the chair opposite him, her eyes pained and pleading. 'Can't you say I'm not well?'

His return gaze carried exasperation. 'That's quite impossible, Judith. Margaret is giving this party for *you*!'

Judith detested conflict and open confrontation of any sort. But her nerves were wearing thin over the situation and she found herself giving vent to her feelings for Margaret for once.

'No, she isn't,' she snapped. 'She can't stand a bar of me. She's giving the party for *you*, Raymond, her beloved big brother.'

Raymond's expression was one of impatience. 'I know you two don't exactly hit it off, but at least she's trying.'

'She certainly is. *Very* trying. She's hated me from soon after I came here to nurse your mother.'

'Really, Judith, how can you say that? Mother's illness was a big strain on the whole family. If Margaret was a bit short with you sometimes, it was prompted by worry.'

Judith could not trust herself to answer, looking down at the rug to hide her frustration.

Short! Margaret had been downright hostile from the moment it had become apparent that Mrs Pascoll had taken a real fancy to her new nurse. Even Judith's seven years of dedicated nursing and look-

ing after Raymond's increasingly frail mother hadn't
tempered the animosity from his sister.

When Mrs Pascoll had died a few months back,
and Raymond had asked Judith to marry him, all hell
had really broken loose. Admittedly, Judith herself
had found his proposal a shock, so she could almost
understand Margaret's feelings on the matter.

Judith had refused at first, but Raymond had been
persistent and persuasive. They liked each other,
he'd argued. They liked doing the same quiet things:
reading, music, movies, the theatre.

Romantic love, such as it was, was for teenagers,
he'd pointed out sensibly. True love was based more
on companionship than passion. They could grow to
truly love each other once they were married. He
was sure of it. He had also promised her at least one
child—another winning argument with Judith. She
would never have seriously considered a childless
marriage. Not at her age.

Raymond's wealth had not been a major factor in
her decision at all, yet when she'd finally consented
to his proposal his sister had accused her of being a
fortune-hunter. It was ironic that Margaret herself
had, the previous year, married a much younger
Latin-lover type with more looks than money, the
complete antithesis of Margaret, who had more
money than looks. Though Margaret pretended to be
happy with Mario, Judith was convinced Raymond's
sister was as miserable as ever.

Raymond's most convincing argument for
Judith's marrying him, however, had been that she
could keep her own bedroom. He was not a highly

sexed man, he'd explained. Not sexless, mind. Just not one driven by carnal needs. He'd confessed to Judith that for some years he'd had an arrangement with a lady-friend of his, whom he visited every couple of weeks. They were not in love, he'd assured her, and he would naturally terminate this intimacy once he was an engaged man.

It suited Judith very well not to have a husband driven by carnal needs. That kind of passion was something she could well live without. It made her shudder just to think of it. All Judith wanted from life these days was a peaceful existence. The last thing she wanted was emotional upheaval and traumatic confrontations. But seeing Alex again would bring both!

'This party Margaret's throwing tonight,' Raymond said, 'is her way of holding out an olive branch to you, Judith. You must come,' he ordered, 'no matter what.'

She looked up and studied Raymond. He was leaning back in the bulky armchair, a quietly autocratic figure, his pipe resting in the corner of his mouth.

He was not a handsome man. His sandy hair was receding, his face was long, his nose sharp, his eyes pale grey and piercing. On either side of his mouth deep grooves ran from his cheeks to his chin.

Despite these unprepossessing physical features, however, Raymond exuded a certain attraction which had nothing to do with his looks. Perhaps it came from the power which went hand in hand with wealth. Raymond was a very rich man. He also had a strong and decisive character which Judith both appreciated and had learnt to rely upon.

'You really can't avoid the issue, Judith,' he insisted logically. 'Why, exactly, are you so upset at the prospect of meeting Alexander Fairchild again? And why do you call him a rotten bastard?'

Raymond removed his pipe and gazed steadily at her, waiting for an answer.

Judith was silent. She sat stiffly, shifting her eyes towards the fire to avoid his penetrating regard. The flames danced before her but she did not see them.

'Were you lovers at some stage?' he asked.

'No!' she denied hotly while throwing him an apprehensive glance.

'There's no need to shout. I don't expect you to be a virgin, Judith, at the age of twenty-nine.'

Her blush took them both by surprise. She'd meant to tell Raymond; had been waiting for the right moment. But it hadn't presented itself yet.

'Good God,' he muttered. 'Why didn't you tell me?'

Judith's chin lifted in an odd defiance. 'Does it matter? I thought men of your generation liked their brides to be virgins on their wedding night. I mean...I thought you'd be pleased.'

'To be honest, I'm more surprised than pleased. You're such a good-looking woman. And you *were* engaged once before, weren't you? And not to a man of my...er...generation. I always imagined most young couples slept together before they married these days.'

'Well, Simon and I didn't,' she said quite sharply,

piqued that Raymond seemed to be finding fault in her virginity. 'Our courtship took place while he was in hospital, recovering after a car accident. By the time he was fit and well and able to make love, we were engaged, and I...I wanted to wait. It was only going to be for another short month and Simon said he didn't mind. He said it would make our marriage all the more special.'

Tears pricked at her eyes as she remembered him saying that, and the warm, understanding kiss which had followed. She knew he'd been frustrated by then, but he'd been prepared to wait. *She'd* been the one who hadn't been able to wait in the end.

And it had cost Simon his life.

That overwhelming sense of guilt swamped her, fiercer than it had been for years. Dear God, would she never forget? Or forgive herself?

One thing was for certain. She would never forgive Alexander Fairchild. The man was as good as guilty of murder in her opinion. She hated him with a passion, hated him for doing what he'd done to her, and to Simon.

A silence had fallen in the room, the only sound the flames crackling in the hearth.

'You must have had some sort of relationship with Fairchild,' Raymond resumed at last with relentless logic, 'or he wouldn't be able to turn you inside out like this.'

'He was Simon's best friend,' she choked out, as though that explained everything.

'So?' Raymond was clearly puzzled. 'That doesn't make much sense, Judith. Look, I know you were engaged to this Simon person, and that he was killed in a motor accident a couple of days before your wedding. But what does Fairchild's being his best friend have to do with that? Your fiancé was alone in the car, wasn't he?'

'Yes.'

'Then I don't understand. Why don't you try to make me understand, Judith?'

Shame compelled her to lie, plus the knowledge that Raymond would never understand or condone the truth. Not that she could blame him. She'd never understood or condoned it herself.

'Simon and Alexander had a violent argument that night,' she explained, running her tongue over dry lips. 'When Simon sped off crazily in the car, Alexander knew he was drunk and upset, but he...he didn't try to stop him. He was directly responsible for the accident and Simon's death, and I'll never, ever forgive him!'

A frown creased Raymond's high forehead. 'What was the argument about?'

'What?'

'The argument between Fairchild and your fiancé. What was it about?'

'Oh...er...I don't really know. There was a lot of shouting and a scuffle, then Simon drove off. What does it matter what it was about now? All I know is that Alexander was to blame for Simon's death.'

'You really think so?'

'I *know* so! Why do you think I don't want to go tonight? Why I can't bear to be in the same room as him?'

Two totally exasperated eyes looked straight at her. 'I never thought you were a fool, Judith, and I'm sure you're not. I can well understand how distressed you must have been at the time of your fiancé's death. But distress does have a way of distorting things in one's mind. With the passing of the years, surely you can see now that Mr Fairchild was not to blame for the accident itself? A man is master of his own destiny. If your fiancé was drunk, he should have refrained from driving.'

Judith opened her mouth to protest but Raymond swept any objection aside.

'Don't forget how you originally met the man,' he went on stolidly. 'In hospital...after a car crash. Doesn't sound like your Simon was the most sensible driver in the world. I think you've harboured an unfair grudge against Fairchild all these years, Judith, and it's high time you put it aside.'

With a pompous flick of his wrist, Raymond checked the time on his wristwatch. 'It is now six forty-three, my dear, and we are expected at eight. Let's hear no more nonsense. Go and put on one of those glamorous gowns you've been buying lately. I want to be the envy of everyone there with my beautiful fiancée on my arm.'

Judith stared at Raymond. He actually meant it. He expected her to simply brush aside her distress as easily as he had and go to the party. He probably expected her to smile at Alexander and act as if nothing had ever happened between them.

He must have seen her shock for he suddenly leant forward and took her hands in his. 'Come now,

Judith, you can't honestly expect me to ring Margaret up at the last minute and say you won't be going. She would never understand.'

Judith nodded slowly. It was hopeless. She would have to go and that was all there was to it.

'I *am* right, you know,' Raymond insisted. 'Your antagonism towards Fairchild is all out of proportion. Time has distorted things in your mind. When you see him again, you'll recognise that. But if you find he still upsets you in any way, then simply avoid him. All I ask is that you be tactful. Now off you go like the sensible girl you are and get ready.'

Judith suppressed a sigh and rose automatically.

'I'll bet Fairchild has hardly given *you* a second thought in all this time,' Raymond added with cold logic.

Those last words hit home, right to the core of her heart. He was right. No doubt Alexander *hadn't* given her a second thought. She hadn't been a real person to him, merely a weapon in his need for vengeance.

'You're quite right, Raymond,' she said with a fierce hardening of her heart. 'Quite right. Thank you for pointing that out to me.'

Judith turned and moved purposefully across the drawing room and out into the foyer, her heels clicking on the marble floor.

Damn you, Alexander Fairchild, she was thinking angrily. Why did you have to show up in my life again now? *Now*, when I'm on the verge of finally finding some happiness and peace of mind. Why couldn't you have stayed in the past, a guilty ghost locked away for ever, together with my night of shame?

Fury and frustration carried Judith swiftly across the spacious foyer, but as she put her foot on the first step of the ornately carved staircase and her eyes lifted to follow the luxurious curve of peacock-blue carpet a disturbing memory struck. Her foot froze, her hand reaching out to curl tightly over the ornately carved knob at the bottom of the balustrade.

She'd been coming down such a staircase when she'd first seen him...

Judith shook herself violently. Her hand released its tormented hold and she continued her ascent, determined not to give in to the maudlin memories that had begun crowding around the edge of her mind. But it was difficult.

At the top of the staircase, she halted again, groaning as she realised the house itself was working against her. It kept reminding her of that other lavishly furnished house, the one to which Simon had taken her a week before their wedding.

Judith had known he came from a well-to-do farming family, but she still hadn't been prepared for the splendour of his home, or the cool sophistication of his mother and sister. Everything had been so overwhelming that first day that she'd found herself acting far more gauchely than she ever had before. Tongue-tied, too.

Simon's father had been quite nice to her, but his mother and sister had let her know, with cleverly disguised barbs, that they thought her highly unsuitable to be Simon's wife. They'd also managed to make her feel hugely indebted to them for paying for the wedding, even though she hadn't asked or expected them to. They'd insisted. Frankly, she would have much preferred a small, quiet ceremony in Shyness.

Judith had tried to dismiss their rudeness and cloak herself in Simon's love, reminding herself constantly that she was marrying him, not his family, and they would live in Simon's lovely little unit in Shyness, not out here in this daunting country mansion.

But then Alexander had arrived, and even the security blanket of her love for Simon had been snatched away. Judith could still remember walking down that staircase with its deep red carpet and the exquisite Chinese rug lying across the bottom.

She'd been putting her foot on that rug when the doorbell had rung. Not wanting to meet another new face that first day, she'd scuttled halfway back up the stairs before Simon's voice had halted her midflight.

'Where on earth are you running off to, Judith? That will probably be Alex. Wait on! Surely you want to meet our best man?'

She waited. Simon strode across the foyer to fling open the front door.

'Alex! Great to see you again, old man. Come in, come in!'

Simon gave his friend a big bear hug, thumping him on the back. He was always like that. Warm. Affable. Not afraid to show his affection, like some men.

Alexander grimaced at first, as though he didn't like being hugged. For a split second, he looked as if he would pull away, but then he glanced up over Simon's shoulder and spotted Judith on the stairs.

He stared at her.

She stared right back, and her heart skittered to a faltering halt.

He wasn't as handsome as Simon in the classical sense. His features were harsher, creating angles and shadows on his face which Judith found instantly, stunningly attractive. As dark as Simon was fair, Alexander's ruggedly tanned face projected a masculine maturity which Simon's pretty-boy looks lacked.

Simon had told her Alexander was the same age as himself—twenty-five—but he looked much older. There was a knowingness about his eyes as well, those penetratingly intelligent black eyes which rooted Judith to the spot on the stairs, seeming to see right into her soul—a soul which was in danger of damnation from the first moment they met.

His intense scrutiny seemed to go on for ever, yet it probably lasted only a few brief moments. It was long enough, however, for Judith to know that her love for Simon was a cruel illusion. Here was a man who could move her more with a look than her fiancé could with the most intimate of kisses.

When he finally looked away, Judith swayed, clutching wildly at the balustrade for support. She felt as if someone had stabbed her, so sharp was the constriction in her chest. A fierce flush spread over her cheeks, testimony to the overheated state of the blood which suddenly rushed through her veins.

'Judith!' Simon called. 'Come down here and meet Alex. Yes, right now,' he insisted when she hesitated in her fluster. 'She's a little shy, is my Judith,' he explained to his silent friend. 'But that's why I love her so. No more blonde bimbos for me, Alex. I'm a changed man.'

How dreadful those next few days were. How confused she was. Simon was even more attentive and loving to her, and she simply could not bring herself to call off their engagement.

If only she had someone she could confide in...

But she was alone in Australia. Her family had emigrated from England when she was a child, but her older sister, Helen, had returned to England on a holiday and subsequently married there. When her father had died of a coronary two years ago, her mother had returned to London to live with Helen. She hadn't had the money to fly over for the wedding. Besides, Helena had been eight months pregnant.

No, there was no one to confide in. No one to warn her that what she was feeling for Alexander Fairchild had brought down kings, and kingdoms. Only afterwards would Judith appreciate that mindless passion always exacted a price. At the time, she convinced herself that once the wedding was over and Alexander was out of their lives everything would be all right.

She did her best to keep out of his way that week, aware of the dangerous nature of her feelings, but he seemed to seek her out deliberately, as keen on her company as she was terrified of his. To give herself credit, she did make sure she was never alone with him, but that didn't stop the longing. Or the dark desires. Her dreams were haunted by his presence, fiercely erotic dreams in which she went further than she'd gone with Simon. Much, much further.

Once and only once, Judith allowed herself the luxury of staring openly at him while he was deep in conversation with Simon's sister. But, unexpectedly, Alexander suddenly glanced across the room and straight into her hungry gaze. She immediately wrenched her eyes away and fled the room, thoroughly ashamed of herself. Had he seen the lust lurking in her soul? she agonised. Had he seen the shameful truth?

Oh, yes, he'd seen, she soon accepted. And was already plotting how to use it for his own vicious ends.

'Judith, what are you doing standing up there, staring into space?' Raymond's sharp words snapped her back to the present. 'We'll be late.'

Judith's face betrayed nothing, but her heart was still thudding with her distressing memories. How on earth was she going to bear seeing that man again?

One look at the stern male face below made her see that she would simply *have* to see him. There was no other way out, unless she wanted to risk her relationship with Raymond.

Pride came to the rescue, demanding that she not

let Alexander Fairchild destroy her life and her
peace of mind a second time. Raymond was a good
man and they would have a good marriage. If bells
didn't ring when he kissed her, then so much the
better. Bells had certainly rung when Alexander had
kissed her, but they'd never been going to turn into
wedding bells. They'd tolled a different bell, leaving
her to be crippled for years by guilt and shame.

'I was just going,' she told Raymond with surprising calm. 'It won't take me long to get ready.'

See, she told herself as she swept down the hallway and into her bedroom. You can handle this.
You're different now. You're an adult, not some
silly, impressionable young girl. He won't get to you
a second time. You simply won't let him!

CHAPTER TWO

JUDITH'S bedroom was the last on the right-hand side of the upstairs hall. Its one large window looked out over the pool and showed a glimpse of Sydney Harbour through the tall trees which lined the back yard. The furniture in the room was dark and elegant, and of good quality walnut, the furnishings equally elegant, in rich cream and apricot colours.

Despite its sophisticated decor, it looked like a young girl's room, for it was full of soft toys of every shape, colour and size. Most of them were bears, sitting in rows along the wall and on every available shelf. But there was also a pair of white rabbits perched on the armrests of the armchair under the window, and a huge pink elephant filling one corner. A long sausage dog called Woofa lay across the end of her bed, and a huge St Bernard called Berni stood guard next to the door.

Judith's pride and joy, however, was her prized panda which shared her bed, getting under the sheets with her at night and lying contentedly against her pillows during the day. Peter Panda had been a present from her father on her eighth birthday, and had proved to be a great comfort to her in moments of loneliness or distress. She loved the feel of his velvet-soft fur, and his wonderful ability to listen to her complaints and confessions without a single critical word.

Judith had added to her collection of silent comforters during her growing-up years whenever she had money of her own. Each toy had been selected for its extra-soft feel and the expression of love and sweet sympathy in its eyes. Whenever she looked at them and held them, Judith instantly felt better. She believed they were worth their weight in gold, and had saved her a fortune in therapy and medication.

Raymond's mother thought her toys cute. Raymond had simply smiled indulgently when he'd first seen them. Margaret had denounced Judith's collection as neurotic and unhealthy.

'I'll bet she even *talks* to them,' she'd sneered to Raymond one day.

Which, of course, she did.

'You'll never guess who's turned up again,' she told them all as she hurried into her room. 'Alexander Fairchild! But don't worry, I'm not about to make a fool of myself again. Can't talk now. I have to get ready and I'm running late.'

Flinging open the doors of the wardrobe, she ran her eyes over the clothes hanging before her.

Judith had never been a flashy or a sexy dresser, not even back in her days with Simon. Nowadays, her attire was even more conservative. But Raymond was right. She'd been shopping for her honeymoon lately and *had* purchased a couple of outfits which might be described as glamorous. Raymond was going to take her on a South Pacific cruise and had instructed her to buy some clothes suitable for elegant evening dining.

Her hand moved to one such new purchase. Primrose-yellow, it was a deceptively innocent creation if one kept the jacket on. The dress, however, was styled like a petticoat, silky and clinging, with shoe-string straps holding up a bodice that moulded around her breasts like a second skin.

Judith stared at it for a moment, unsure of wearing such a provocative gown in Alexander's presence. Till she reminded herself that her passion for the man had been a one-sided affair, *his* desire all being pretence. She could probably stand naked before him tonight and he wouldn't turn a hair.

Angry defiance took hold of Judith at the thought. She threw the outfit onto the bed then marched into the shower. Some considerable time later, she stood in front of the dressing-table mirror, gnawing away at her bottom lip as she surveyed the dress again, now that it was on her body.

Judith was not a busty girl.

But still...

She gulped at the sight of her tall, slender form encased in that clinging yellow silk. The effect was not only sexy. It was downright seductive!

Despairingly, she dragged on the thigh-length jacket with its long sleeves and high Chinese collar, then took another look. Ah, that was much better. Her braless breasts, and especially her irritatingly hard nipples, were now well covered. No way did she want anyone misinterpreting any unfortunate body language, especially Alexander. She was determined to show him she felt nothing for him any more, nothing except a mild derision and a total lack of interest.

A loud rap on the door made her jump.

'Ten minutes, Judith,' Raymond ordered peremptorily through the door. 'I'll meet you downstairs, at the front door, right on the dot of seven forty-five.'

Judith bristled at Raymond's officiousness, which was silly, because he wasn't being any different from his usual self. He'd always been a bit bossy, and punctuality was an obsession with him. Being a trained nurse, she was used to schedules and appointed times. Usually, she found them comforting. But tonight, for some reason, she was irritated by Raymond's autocratic attitude.

'I'll be ready, Raymond,' she called back, gritting her teeth as she did so.

Turning back to the mirror, Judith set about doing her hair, deft fingers whisking her long chestnut-brown locks up at the sides, and anchoring it on top of her head with a gold and tortoiseshell comb. The rest she left to tumble halfway down her back, its natural wave demanding no attention other than a quick brush.

She'd already done her make-up, her clear olive complexion needing little adornment, just a brushing of blusher. At night, she always emphasised her large green eyes with mascara and earth-toned eye shadows. Her mouth, which was wide and full, did not really suit red lipsticks, so she generally stuck to browns.

Judith stared at the finished result in the mirror. She looked good. More than good. She looked glamorous, and sultry, and downright sexy.

'What do you think?' she asked her silently watching audience. 'Too provocative? Yes? No? Say something, for pity's sake!' She whirled round to glare into Peter's soulful eyes. 'I know what you're thinking. You think I want him to look at me—just *once*—with real desire in his eyes, don't you? *Don't you?*' she repeated, stalking over to snatch the panda up and shake him.

'Well, maybe I do,' she admitted with a strangled sob, and hugged the panda tightly to her. 'But there's no danger of that happening, Peter. He never really fancied me, not one little bit. He just pretended. He didn't want me. He just wanted revenge!'

It had happened two days before the actual wedding, the night of the big party, when everyone for miles around came to meet Simon's prospective bride. Anyone who was anyone, that was. Simon's family only mixed with the best in country society.

Judith felt ill-at-ease all night in her simple green party dress, especially when Simon kept leaving her alone for great chunks of time on end. She'd never been one for mixing at parties, not having been blessed with Simon's easy charm. Several times, she felt Alexander's intense gaze upon her, but she steadfastly resisted looking back at him.

By the time the antique clock on the wall in the main living room struck midnight, the party was in full swing. Drinks flowed. A lot of people were merry, and many were downright drunk. A sozzled Simon had just reappeared after another absence, only to immediately excuse himself again. He'd said he was going to get her a drink, despite her protest that she didn't want another. She's already had far too many glasses of champagne on her relatively empty stomach, and her head was beginning to spin.

Five minutes went by, then another, and he did not return. She was about to go in search of him when Alexander appeared by her side, a glass of white wine in his hand.

'Simon asked me to bring you this,' he said. 'His mother wanted him for something. He shouldn't be too long. Do you mind if I stay and talk to you for a while?'

His eyes locked with hers and immediately she was lost. 'I...no, I...I don't mind,' she said shakily.

They talked and talked. Simon didn't come back and Judith scarcely noticed. Alexander told her how he and Simon had become best friends while doing an economics degree together at Sydney Uni a few years before, but that whereas Simon had gone on to a position as a trainee executive in a large insurance company he had had to give up his own banking career to return to run the family farm near Goulburn. His father had tragically lost both his legs at the knees when he'd been run over by the tractor.

Judith found him a man of great depth, not at all what she'd expected. She would have preferred to find him shallow and insincere, unworthy of her mad longings—someone she could despise and thereby kill her infatuation.

But any despising was not to come till much later. That night she found nothing to despise, only to desire.

An hour passed. Alexander went in search of the still missing Simon, only to return alone, a dark frown on his face. Abruptly, he took the now empty wineglass from her hand and asked her to dance.

What madness! What joy! She could touch him and no one could condemn her. She could revel in his nearness, for she was safe in the company of others.

But he steered her away, first out onto the terrace and then down into the extensive grounds. When they reached a secluded spot behind a hedge, he swung her to a stop and just stared down at her. She was both afraid and thrilled by the look in his eyes. When he kissed her, the dam of desire she'd tried so hard to bottle up spilled wide open and all her passion for him poured forth.

Oh, such a torrent of feeling it was. Such a flood of longing. She was just swept away. Within minutes he had her on the ground, her clothes pushed aside. She was panting beneath him, eyes squeezed shut, mouth agape.

Alexander was only a second away from total possession, Judith clinging to him in abandoned submission, when the cold clarity of Simon's voice froze her with shame.

'You lying, cheating little bitch!'

Alexander rose quickly, pulling down her skirt and adjusting his own clothing with amazing speed. Judith just lay there on the grass, stricken with shame. Her eyes were round with shock. How could you have done this? her conscience cried piteously.

Simon was no longer looking at her but glaring at Alexander, wild fury in his eyes. His arm swung round with violent intent, but Alexander warded off the blow with his elbow. Simon swayed, and Judith saw that his cheeks were flushed and his eyes bloodshot. He was very, very drunk, she realised as she scrambled to her feet at last.

'Please, Simon,' she said pathetically, grasping at his arm. 'I...I'm sorry. I—'

He struck her. A savage blow to the side of her head, sending her sprawling. Alexander grabbed her before she fell to the ground, then whipped round to face Simon. 'I'll kill you, you bastard,' he threatened. 'Touch her again and I'll kill you.'

'She's all yours, dear friend,' came the sneering retort. 'Screw her to death for all I care.'

Simon lurched across the lawn and into his blue Aston Martin. The car burst into life and screeched off down the drive, sending a shower of gravel scattering at their feet. They didn't even have time to speak to each other before they heard the sound of the crash and saw the fire-ball in the distance.

Simon's family and friends never found out why he'd driven off so crazily to his death. Alexander didn't confess to anything. Judith had begged him not to. And when he announced that he wasn't able to stay for the funeral, a sudden downturn in his father's health calling him home, she thought it was for the best. How could she possibly stand by his side at Simon's graveside?

By the time Simon was buried, her guilt was overwhelming. She knew then that it would take her a long time to get over what she'd done. Her only comfort was the knowledge that Alexander must truly love her to have betrayed his best friend like that, as she must truly love him.

He'd promised to come back and get her in a couple of days. She was counting the moments till his arrival, wanting to get right away, away from the misery in that home, away from the scene of their crime, so to speak.

But it wasn't Alexander who came. It was his sister, Karen...

Judith was lying down in her room when she was told there was someone on the front veranda to see her. The visitor refused to come inside.

Puzzled, Judith went downstairs and out on to the veranda, gazing with curiosity upon the pretty dark-haired young woman waiting there. She'd been crying, Judith noted.

'You're Judith Anderson, Simon's fiancée?' the girl asked.

'Yes.' But who on earth was *she*?

The girl pulled out a crumpled handkerchief from a plain black handbag and blew her nose. A thick lock of hair fell across her eyes and she agitatedly pushed it aside. The gesture reminded Judith of someone, but she couldn't quite put her finger on who.

'I'm sorry,' the girl blubbered. 'I'm really sorry.' Then she totally lost control and the tears flooded anew.

Judith took her elbow and led her to the long seat against the wall. 'Let's sit down,' she said gently, 'and you can tell me what you're sorry about, plus who you are.'

The girl lifted her tear-stained face, her brown eyes widening. 'Oh, that's right. I forgot. I...I'm Karen Fairchild, Alex's sister.'

Of course, Judith realised. The same forehead and hair—hair that was always falling forward.

'If only I'd known,' Karen blurted out. 'I'd never have told Alex. Never! But he was insisting that I come to your wedding, and I just couldn't.'

With that she buried her head in her hands and wept some more.

Judith's thoughts were a whirlwind of confusion. What terrible thing was this girl trying to tell her?

'What shouldn't you have told your brother?' she asked slowly, already dreading the answer.

The girl looked hard at Judith now and the weeping stopped. 'I'm not sure you'll want to hear this, you having loved Simon. But I loved him too and I'll never forgive Alex if he was to blame for Simon's death. He didn't say much when he came home but I knew. I just knew he'd done something.'

Judith stood up abruptly and walked over to the edge of the veranda, her heart thudding heavily in her chest. She took a deep breath to calm herself and turned to face her visitor.

'Let me get this clear, Karen. You were in love with Simon?'

The girl nodded.

'And Alex found out?'

'That's part of it...'

'So what's the other part?'

Karen looked upset, as though she wished she hadn't started this confession. 'I suppose I'll have to tell you it all now,' she said unhappily, then fell silent.

Judith waited for her to go on, unable to trust herself to speak. The feeling of foreboding was fierce within her heart.

'Last Easter,' the girl began at last, 'Simon came down to stay at the farm for a few days. Alex had to work most of the time and I...well, it fell to me mostly to entertain Simon.

'It wasn't Simon's fault. Really and truly. I threw myself at him and he...well... I knew he didn't really love me, that it was just...you know. But I didn't care. I was mad about him. I even told him it was safe. I had this silly idea that you couldn't get pregnant the first time. By the time I realised I was, I knew there was no chance between Simon and me. He'd been gone for weeks and hadn't answered any of my letters. Then Alex got a note saying he'd met this great girl and was going to marry her...'

Karen looked wretched and Judith just stared at her.

She was not feeling what she should be. She was not shocked over Simon's less than gallant conduct, just increasingly terrified of hearing what she feared would come next. Her expression must have revealed some of her turmoil for Karen rose and came forward and took her hand in a gesture of sympathy.

'I'm truly sorry,' she murmured. 'I know this

must be hurting you, but I have to make you understand. I have to know.'

'Go on,' said Judith coldly, drawing her hand away. No one warmed to the bearer of ill tidings.

'I had an abortion,' came her reluctant admission. 'An aunt of mine in Sydney helped without telling the rest of the family, but when I came home I had a type of nervous breakdown. Everyone tried to find out what was wrong but I never told them.

'Then the invitation to your wedding came and Alex thought it would cheer me up to go. I couldn't cope with that and refused to come. The night before Alex left to come here he tried to persuade me again. I'm afraid I became hysterical and told him the truth.

'I'll never forget the look on his face. It was horrible. I tried explaining that Simon wasn't to blame but he didn't believe me. Alex is not one to forget or forgive. I knew he'd do something awful, and he did, didn't he? Simon's dead...'

All the blood had drained from Judith's face. Karen's words were almost too distressing to contemplate, the truth behind them starkly plain for Judith to see. Alexander had used her, used her to gain revenge. Maybe he wasn't a murderer in the literal sense of the word, but he was very definitely to blame for the circumstances leading up to Simon's death. She could well have understood his beating Simon up, but to involve an innocent party...

Innocent? How could she call herself that? She hadn't been innocent. She'd allowed herself to be seduced, had wallowed in the moments of betrayal almost as much as Alexander had. Even poor dead Simon could not claim total innocence. He should have protected his friend's kid sister, not slept with her.

The only true innocent in all this was the girl standing in front of her, who could be no more than seventeen. She didn't deserve to suffer any more. Judith knew her own life was destroyed. She could not destroy Karen's further.

'Tell me I'm wrong,' the girl pleaded. 'Tell me Alex wasn't in any way to blame for Simon's death. I've been so afraid.'

Judith gathered all her mental and emotional strength. 'Let me assure you, Karen,' she lied staunchly, 'that Alexander had nothing to do with Simon's death. Simon was entirely at fault. He went joyriding in his own sports car while drunk. He lost control on some gravel on a corner, skidded off the road and crashed into a tree. Alexander had nothing to do with it. He and Simon had been getting along famously all week so Simon must have made him understand what happened where you and he were concerned.

'For pity's sake don't accuse him of anything. Let it go, Karen. Go home and let it go. Now, if you'll excuse me I must go and get ready to go home too. I have to catch tonight's train back to Sydney.'

She didn't wait to see the relief in the girl's face, walking back inside like some half-charged robot. She went upstairs to her room, where she sat down and wrote to Alex, telling him she was sorry but she

knew they would never find happiness after Simon's
death and she didn't want to see him ever again.

It wasn't till much later that she realised what a
futile gesture it had been. She'd thought she was
protecting Karen at the time, but of course
Alexander would never have come after her. The
only thing she'd gained by writing that letter was
that she'd started taking control of her life again
after being severely out of control since meeting
him.

After posting the letter, she'd taken the train back
to Sydney that night, quit her job and her shared flat,
then accepted the first live-in nursing job she could
find. She'd been installed in the Pascoll home within
thirty-six hours of arriving at Central Station.

Judith shook herself back to the present, taking some
comfort this time not from hugging Peter Panda but
from the harsh memories themselves. Remembering
what had happened would keep her on her guard
against Alexander tonight.

Not that she really had anything to fear. Alex's
own conscience should keep him at bay this time. It
would take an especially wicked individual to ignore
his own ignominy and act as if it had never happened.

Judith didn't doubt that Alexander was going to
get quite a shock when he saw her tonight. And in
a way that gave her a perverse sense of satisfaction.
The man should never be allowed to forget what he
had done. When he saw her he would be forced to
remember. She might even slip in the odd barb or

two, make him suffer a little as she had suffered over the years. At the same time she would give the impression that she had well and truly recovered and was on the verge of a superbly happy life.

It would not be easy to put all that across, but she was determined to do it.

But when she placed Peter back on her bed and turned to pick up her tapestry evening purse from her dressing-table she became aware of dozens of black beady eyes following her every movement. For the first time in her life, Judith found no comfort in her friends' presence. They seemed to be looking at her with worry, not warmth. Peter especially.

'I'll be careful,' she said at last. 'I promise.'

And, steeling herself, she left the sanctuary of her bedroom and hurried along the hall in the direction of the stairs.

Raymond was already waiting for her at the door, looking a little agitated, probably because she was a few minutes late. His eyes lifted to watch her descent and when her jacket flapped open the shock on his face was evident.

His reaction annoyed her. 'Don't you like the way I look?' she was driven to ask when she joined him.

'What? Oh, yes...of course.' He gave her another long, frowning look. 'You look quite...striking.'

'Thank you, Raymond,' she returned coolly, irritated that his admiration had been so slow in coming. If you could call the way he was looking at her admiration. His expression was more like one of troubled speculation. Judith sighed inwardly. She certainly didn't seem to be finding favour with him tonight.

Not that she could really blame him. She wasn't being her usual quiet, amenable self, that was for sure.

Feeling suddenly guilty, she linked an affectionate arm through his and gave him a peck on the cheek. 'Don't look so worried,' she said soothingly. 'I'll be nice to Margaret tonight, and I promise I won't make a scene with Mr Fairchild.'

Raymond relaxed a little and patted her hand. 'Thank God for that. I'm having important business dealings with the man and I wouldn't like anything to interfere with them.'

Important business dealings?

Judith blinked her confusion. Raymond's business was a large frozen food company inherited from his father, it's main products being vegetables. His life was running this company, and he ran it very profitably. When he'd told Judith about his having to put off a business dinner with Alexander and invite him to the party tonight instead, she'd assumed he was signing him up to supply fresh vegetables. Alexander was, after all, a farmer.

'I'm not sure I understand,' she said. 'What kind of important dealings?'

'I want to buy some land from him,' Raymond explained as he opened the front door. 'I'm going into the crop-growing business myself. It'll be much cheaper in the long run than buying supplies from various farmers.'

'You mean you're buying Alexander's farm?'

'What on earth are you talking about, Judith?'

'Oh,' she said. 'Oh, I see. Alexander's given up farming and gone back into banking.'

Now Raymond was the one who looked puzzled. '*Banking?* Fairchild's no banker. He's in real estate. Owns great tracts of rich land in the Riverina and along the Southern coastline.'

'But…but…'

'Come, Judith,' he said, ushering her out of the door. 'No more talk of Fairchild. It's nearly eight. You know how I do so hate to be late. Luckily, I've already got the car out.'

CHAPTER THREE

THE night was cold outside. Sydney in August was still nippy, and often windy. Spring was nearly a month away.

Judith shivered as they hurried down the front path and over to the waiting grey Mercedes. It was all very well for Raymond to dismiss Alexander from his mind. *Judith's* mind had never been that kind. She'd tried to dismiss him over the last seven years, but had never really succeeded.

Now he'd been forcibly thrust to the forefront of her thoughts again but he wasn't even the same man she remembered. How on earth had he gone from being a small-time farmer to a high-powered real-estate man in only seven years? It seemed impossible. Unless he'd inherited money.

Or married it...

The thought of Alexander marrying had never occurred to her before, which was crazy. Why shouldn't he be married? The man was now thirty-two years old.

She ached to ask Raymond if he was aware of Alexander's marital status, but knew it would be too revealing a question. Her own inner churnings over the matter were revealing enough as it was. Why should she care if he was married or not? She hated the man, didn't she?

Raymond drove as he always did. In silence. He needed to concentrate, he'd told her the first night he'd taken her out to the ballet—about a year ago. And she always obliged by not indulging in any distracting chatter.

Normally, she found this quite relaxing, but tonight it gave her too much time to think. What would have happened, she agonised, if Alexander's sister hadn't told her the truth? Would she have run after Alexander when he hadn't shown up as promised? What excuse would he have made not to have any more to do with her? Guilt?

Perhaps. Probably. And she would have believed him. Her own guilt had been crushing.

Her head whirled and her thoughts tumbled on. What would have happened, too, if Simon hadn't followed them that night and caught them in the act? Judith didn't believe Alexander's intention had been to cause Simon's death. She believed he had come to the house that first day intending to have things out with his supposed best friend. She'd witnessed his tension during that first hug.

But then he'd spied Judith, stupid, smitten Judith, standing there drooling open-mouthed over him, and his plan had immediately changed from open confrontation to devious revenge. He would seduce Simon's silly fiancée, maybe even make *her* pregnant, as Simon had Karen. He would destroy Simon's happiness, uncaring if he destroyed hers at the same time.

Ruthless, he'd been, in his vengeance. Quite ruthless.

Admittedly, there'd been evidence of some regret afterwards. He'd seemed genuinely distressed by Simon's death. But it had been too late then, hadn't it? Too late for Simon. Too late for herself...

Judith's stomach churned as she thought of all she'd suffered at his hands. God, but she hated him, hated him with the same kind of passion which had once filled her with desire. The only desire she had now was to see him in hell—the same hell he'd consigned her to all those years ago!

'We're ten minutes late,' Raymond pronounced as he turned the Mercedes into Margaret's street, a very fashionable address in Hunter's Hill.

'We'll still be the first ones here, Raymond,' she said, knowing from experience that when people said parties started at eight most of the guests turned up at nine, or later.

The car rolled to a stop in front of the lovely old two-storeyed home Raymond had bought and presented to Margaret as a wedding present, the absence of other cars at the kerb or in the driveway confirming Judith's opinion that they were the first arrivals.

'Mr Fairchild doesn't know I'm your fiancée, does he?' she asked as they made their way up the steep front steps.

'I certainly never told him,' Raymond replied. 'And there are no photographs of you on my desk. You know I don't go in for that kind of sentimentality,' he said firmly, and rang the doorbell.

Judith frowned at this last remark as they waited

silently for the doorbell to be answered. Were all men as practical and pragmatic as Raymond? Was sentiment a strictly female prerogative?

Surely not, she decided. Simon had been a very warm and sensitive man. It had been the first thing she'd noticed and loved about him.

Judith herself felt things very deeply and was quickly moved to sympathy for the plights of others. That was why she'd decided to be a nurse in the first place. Unfortunately, however, sometimes she felt things too deeply.

After she'd completed her training as a nurse, she'd worked in the Aids ward for a while, but had finally had to request a transfer to a general ward after breaking down once too often. She'd been just too heartbroken at her patients' suffering and their lack of any real hope.

Over the years she'd learnt to control her emotions better, especially in public, but she was still a softie underneath, crying copious tears at sad movies. Letters from her mother or her sister could start her off, as did pictures of neglected and abused animals in newspapers. She usually hid her tears, however, turning to her toy friends for comfort rather than real people.

Raymond would be embarrassed if she ever blubbered all over him. It was as well, Judith decided now, that she was to keep her own bedroom after they were married. At least there she had Peter to blubber all over. He didn't mind one bit!

'For pity's sake stop worrying about Fairchild,' Raymond snapped suddenly, breaking into her thoughts. 'He might not even turn up. You know how people are about parties these days.'

Judith's heart leapt momentarily at the possibility that she still might escape the awful prospect of coming face to face with Alexander again. But somehow she didn't think fate was going to be that kind.

'He'll show up,' she muttered.

Raymond shot her a sharp look. 'You promised you wouldn't make a scene.'

Judith sighed. 'I won't, Raymond. But I'm not going to pretend I'm thrilled about seeing him again.'

'Just don't do or say anything that might jeopardise my business dealings with him.'

Judith fell silent, hurt by Raymond's total insensitivity towards her feelings on this matter. It showed her just where she rated with the man she'd agreed to marry. She would always play second fiddle to his business. She would never come first. Never.

Judith's unhappy thoughts were scattered by the opening of the front door and the appearance of Margaret's sleazily handsome husband. Admittedly, Mario did cut a fine figure of a man in the black silk-blend dinner suit he was wearing, but there was something infinitely repulsive about his oily, slicked-back hair and slightly feminine features, not to mention his overly effusive manner.

'Ray! Judy! Marge will be so pleased you're finally here.' His Latin accent was attractive but his penchant for nicknames annoyed Judith to death. 'It wouldn't do for the guests of honour to be too late, would it?'

He babbled on as he ushered them both into the hallway. The central heating, rather stuffy after the crisp air outside, enveloped Judith, causing beads of perspiration to break out on her forehead. She drew a tissue from her purse, dabbing nervously at her face.

'Here, Judy,' he said, stepping round behind her. 'Let me take your jacket. You look hot.'

With one swift movement, deft fingers removed the security of her jacket. Judith glanced apprehensively over her shoulder, only to see two lecherous dark eyes raking over her bosom. She flushed under Mario's lustful stare and turned to Raymond for sanctuary. Swiftly linking her arm through his, she was about to bustle him into the large living room on their left when she was halted by the sight of Margaret floating down the stairs towards them in lavender chiffon.

Dear Lord, what an unattractive woman she was!

Her looks were similar to her brother's, but where he could be described as tall and lean Margaret was skinny and shapeless. Raymond was able to carry off a long face and large nose with distinction. On his sister, they looked horsy. The down-turn of a sour mouth didn't improve things, either.

'How naughty of you to be late, Raymond, love,' she said brushing her brother's cheek with a kiss before flicking cold eyes over Judith. 'My, that's a daring little dress you're wearing tonight, Judith.'

'She has the figure to wear it,' Raymond retorted, surprising Judith with his defence of her. In the past, Margaret's snide remarks had seemed to go right over his head. She smiled her gratitude at him but he didn't smile back, his eyebrows bunching together as he scowled down at her cleavage.

Judith's heart leapt when the front doorbell rang behind her, but it wasn't Alexander who was ushered in. It was a couple she didn't recognise. Frankly, she didn't recognise any of the people who arrived over the next hour, other than Raymond's secretary, who came on her own. A widow in her early forties, Joyce was a pleasant but rather plain woman who had worked for Raymond for eons and was devoted to him.

Judith found herself introduced to distant relatives of Raymond's she'd never met before, then half a dozen business associates and their wives, plus several sophisticated couples who were part of Margaret and Mario's social set.

They all gave Judith a thorough once-over, and once again Judith got the impression she was found wanting as a bride-to-be. Too young for Raymond, their eyes seemed to say. And far too flashy.

But Judith was beyond caring what any of them thought. She stood by Raymond's side near the marble fireplace, smiling plastic smiles and sipping champagne while her whole attention was riveted on the doorway which led back to the front hall. She was watching and waiting for Alexander to arrive, dreading it, yet desperate for it at the same time. There was nothing worse than waiting for something awful to happen. Far better to get it over and done with.

But Alexander didn't arrive. Nine o'clock came and went. The introductions dried up and the party settled into full swing. More champagne flowed. Finger food was served from circling trays. The tone of the background music changed to a dancing beat.

The more sedate guests found chairs and sofas while the young at heart spilled from the main living room into the large family room beyond, where they could dance on the polished wooden floor. Raymond and Judith settled in a corner of the lounge room, along with Margaret and Joyce, while Mario was off dancing and flirting as usual.

Judith wasn't sure if she felt relieved or not by Alexander's non-appearance. There was a tight pain in her chest from holding herself in anticipation of seeing him again which was not at all relaxing. When the sound of the doorbell came again—at least fifteen minutes after the last arrival—she suddenly felt faint. This was him. She just *knew* it.

'Perhaps that's our errant Mr Fairchild,' Raymond whispered in her ear as Margaret rose and went to answer the door. 'I sincerely hope so.'

Judith felt Joyce's eyes on her as she waited in stiff silence for Margaret's return. Why was Raymond's secretary staring at her like that? she wondered. Did she look as pale as she felt? And as petrified?

Please, God, don't let me still feel what I once felt for him, she prayed as she waited. I couldn't bear it.

She stared blankly down into her half-empty glass of champagne, flinching when Raymond abruptly got to his feet.

'Alexander!' he boomed in a hearty greeting. 'You made it. I was beginning to think you weren't coming.'

'I had a business dinner I couldn't get out of,' came the deeply timbred reply. 'I came as soon as I could get away.'

A shudder ran through Judith at the sound of that voice. So utterly male. So impressively mature. It hadn't changed one bit.

Her eyes slowly lifted, following the length of his tall frame, which was casually yet elegantly encased in a beige woollen suit and a black crew-necked sweater. Shock rippled through her when her gaze reached his face, for there he *had* changed.

Never a classically handsome man, the years had etched a brutal harshness on his already sharp features, and he looked every one of his thirty-two years. His once longish, wavy black hair was cut very short on top, the sides slicked ruthlessly back. His skin was weathered and deeply tanned. There were deep lines around his mouth, crow's-feet around his eyes and a smattering of grey at his temples. He looked tough as teak, and every inch the ruthless bastard she'd always believed him to be.

Hard black eyes suddenly met hers, and for a moment he stared at her in total astonishment.

'Judith?' he said, his voice a shocked rasp.

Judith was speechless as she gazed up at him. Nothing had changed, she realised with a sinking heart and a rapidly escalating dread. Nothing…

'You know Judith?' Margaret said, her thin eyebrows arching in surprise.

'Mr Fairchild's an old friend of Judith's,' Raymond supplied into the decidedly thickening atmosphere. 'They haven't seen each other in years. No doubt you're somewhat surprised to find you already know my fiancée, Alexander. I know Judith was a bit taken aback when I dropped your name this evening, weren't you, darling?'

'Indeed I was,' came her amazingly calm reply. It showed Judith she was far more capable of handling the situation than she would ever have expected. Inside she was a mess, but it didn't show on the outside, she realised with enormous relief.

'How are you, Alex?' she asked with cool composure, a light smile playing on her lips. 'You're looking fit and well. Raymond tells me you've gone into real estate.'

'That's right.'

Judith gained some satisfaction from seeing that her adversary was far more rattled than she appeared to be. His nostrils had flared wide at the revelation that she was Raymond's fiancée. Now he was frowning as though he could hardly credit his misfortune in meeting up with her again.

'How did you and Judith come to be friends?' Margaret insisted on knowing. 'Goodness, I hope you're not some long-lost love come to claim Raymond's fiancée at the last moment,' she added, with a dry little laugh.

Judith felt sick at this ironic remark. Love had never come into it. Not even on *her* side. She could see that now. Her feelings for Alexander were exactly the same as they'd been seven years ago. It was lust, not love. One look, and her body still snapped to attention, craving the chemistry only he could evoke. Yet she loathed the man. How perverse could one get?

'Hardly,' Alexander drawled. 'Judith was once engaged to my best friend.'

'Really?' Margaret was all ears. 'I had no idea you were engaged before, Judith. Did you know she was engaged before, Raymond?'

'Yes, of course I did,' he snapped. For once, he was

looking at his sister with irritation. 'Judith doesn't like
to talk about it. Her fiancé was tragically killed in a
road accident a couple of days before the wedding.'

Margaret and Joyce made sympathetic noises while
Judith did her best to stay composed. For Alexander
was looking her over with a decidedly sardonic regard,
as though *she* were the guilty party from the past, not
he. His attitude totally bamboozled her, so much so
that her façde slipped a little, her eyes flashing angrily
at him.

His cold black eyes widened momentarily in return,
then narrowed, his ebony gaze chilling even further as
it roved over her revealing dress. Mario's abrupt in-
trusion into the group brought a welcome distraction
and a measure of relief.

'So who's going to dance with me next?' he asked.
'Marge? No? Joyce? No? Truly, you ladies don't know
how to have fun! What about you, Judy? You *will*?'

His surprise at her accepting his invitation was
quickly supplemented by a wide-eyed glance at her
chest as she rose from the sofa. Judith didn't have to
look down to see how her body was betraying her.
Without looking at Alexander again, she put her hand
in Mario's and let him lead her away into the next
room where several couples were dancing.

To give Mario credit, he was an excellent dancer.
He would have rivalled Rudolph Valentino. But he
was also a compulsive womaniser who never let an
opportunity to practise the art of seduction go by.
Throughout their acquaintance, Judith had made sure
she was never alone with him. Till now.

'Tell me, Judy, why do you marry such an old

man?' he breathed into her ear as he whirled her around. 'Is it just for the money, yes? You will have other lovers as compensation?'

She might have pulled away if he hadn't been holding her so tightly—and if the alternative to staying with him hadn't been worse. Whenever he turned her round she glimpsed Alexander in the other room, chatting away to Margaret of all people. Raymond and Joyce seemed to have disappeared.

'I am not marrying Raymond for his money,' she denied firmly.

'You do not love him,' Mario stated just as firmly.

Her eyes flew upwards to meet his darkly glittering gaze. 'Why do you say that?'

'Because I know. You do not look at him like a woman in love.'

'There are many types of love, Mario.'

'Not for a woman as young and as beautiful as you.'

'There's more to life than sex, too.'

He threw back his head and laughed. 'Not where men my age are concerned.'

'And how old *are* you, Mario?'

'Such a personal question, Judy, my sweet! Shall we say I'm still well on the right side of forty? Which is more than can be said for Raymond.'

'He's only forty-seven,' she defended hotly.

'He acts like he's seventy-seven.'

'I *like* the way Raymond acts.'

Mario frowned down at her. 'Then you're a very strange young woman. But a very beautiful one.'

Judith gasped when he drew her breathtakingly close, his breath hot against her hair. She was just contemplating ending the dance when she glanced over Mario's shoulder and saw Alexander walking towards them with a face like stone. He tapped Mario on the shoulder, fixing cold eyes on Judith as he spoke.

'My turn.'

Mario blinked his surprise for a second, then shrugged and walked off to find another partner, leaving an appalled Judith to be drawn into Alexander's arms.

As though on command from the devil himself, the music suddenly changed to a slower number, with the sort of rhythm just made for lovers. Judith smothered a groan of dismay when Alexander gathered her sickeningly close and began swaying her body in time to the throbbing beat.

Instantly, her heart began to pound, pumping heated blood through her veins. Her skin tingled, goosebumps standing erect on her bare arms. Her nipples, already erect, found perverse pleasure in brushing painfully against the hard wall of his chest.

A dark, erotic excitement ran through Judith and she knew, knew with a certainty that was as shocking as it was sure, that Alexander could do the same thing to her again if he wanted: take her away this very moment to some private place and reduce her to a mindless mess of sexual surrender. Easily. Effortlessly.

Her body had been his to do with as he willed seven years ago. And it was still his.

Her shame in her own weakness was acute. She hated him. Yet still she wanted him, wanted him with a passion that was instantly out of control and totally conscienceless.

It was just as well, she thought despairingly, that their relationship, such as it was, had been a one-sided affair. Otherwise she would be in deep, deep trouble.

At least she had her newly discovered composure to hide behind—so important in the face of her on-going vulnerability to this man. It was to be hoped it would last. Because it was one thing to remain cool while in conversation with him, quite another while dancing in his arms!

CHAPTER FOUR

'WELL, Judith,' Alex murmured as he executed a seductively slow turn. 'It's been a long time, hasn't it?'

'Seven years,' she returned coolly, while doing her best to hold herself away from his body.

But it was impossible. He was too strong for her. Way too strong. On top of that, he seemed determined not to leave a spare inch between them.

'You don't look a day older,' he complimented silkily, the large hand in the small of her back keeping her pressed against him.

'Thank you,' she bit out, willing herself to stay unmoved by the continuous contact of his very male, very hard body.

Once again, she failed. Her body was already in meltdown mode, moulding itself against his, every soft curve seeking out a complementary hardness in his, chest against chest, stomach to stomach, thigh to thigh. The sensation was thrilling, yet chilling.

Dear God, help me...she prayed silently.

'So what have you been doing these past seven years, Judith?'

'Nursing,' came her curt reply.

'Really? All the time? Where?'

'Why do you want to know, Alex?' she asked stiffly.

'Curiosity, I guess. I spent some considerable time trying to find you seven years ago but you'd disappeared so effectively I wasn't successful.'

Judith ground to a halt, shock sending her eyes flying to his. 'You...you tried to find me?'

'What did you expect? Did you think that one pathetic little letter written in a state of emotional distress would keep me away from you?'

'But I...I...'

'You what, Judith? You didn't *want* me to come after you? Oh, I gathered that in the end. I'm not a stupid man. You obviously didn't feel quite as deeply for me as I did for you.'

He started moving her numbed body around the dance-floor again, though it wasn't as numb as her mind. Alex had come after her? But why would he, if all he'd wanted was revenge? Dear God, surely he couldn't have really been in love with her back then? Surely not...

'Not that it matters now,' he continued with chilling indifference. 'Time has a way of healing just about any wound. I'm not in love with you any more. Fact is, I haven't given you a second thought for quite some time. There've been plenty of other women in my life since you.

'But seeing you again tonight *did* make me curious. I've just found out from your fiancé's sister that you were their dearly departed mother's nurse. But where were you nursing before that? I'd love to know—especially where you went after leaving Westmead. Not to work in any of the other hospitals in Sydney. *That* I know.'

'I...I came straight to the Pascoll home,' she told him haltingly while her mind revolved in circles. He'd really come after her... He *had* loved her... But he didn't any more... Plenty of other women in his life since her...

'All that time in just one position?' he asked, disbelief in his voice.

'What? Oh. Yes. I was Mrs Pascoll's nurse for seven years. She had a degenerative disease. She only died a few months back.'

'After which you gave up nursing in favour of being the future Mrs Raymond Pascoll,' he said. 'I see...'

'I doubt it,' Judith snapped.

By the time Maisie had passed on, she had been physically and emotionally exhausted. Nursing the dying woman had been a twenty-four-hour job towards the end. When Raymond had suggested after the funeral that she stay on at the house for a few weeks' much needed rest, she'd been only too happy to agree. And it was during that time that he'd first asked her to marry him.

'I think I see things better than you realise, Judith,' Alex returned smoothly. 'Margaret was amazingly informative about you just now, though I'd warn you not to count her as a friendly future sister-in-law. She even volunteered the news of her mother's generous cash legacy to you.

'She didn't exactly spell out her contempt in words but her tone suggested that beautiful and conscienceless nurses who wangled their way into the affections of their elderly and vulnerable patients for material gain should have unspeakable things done to them.'

Judith was cut to the quick with dismay and hurt. Was there no end to Margaret's jealousy? 'Was it my fault the woman liked me?' she said. 'And it wasn't all that much money, given the size of Mrs Pascoll's estate. Margaret inherited millions. I have no idea why she's so spiteful and vindictive towards me.'

'No? Then you must be blind, Judith. But actually I'm inclined to agree with you about the money, now that I know the extent of your effort. Fifty grand is a nice little nest-egg, but not all that much recompense for seven years' hard labour, especially if you had to put up with Sourpuss at the same time. Being Mrs Raymond Pascoll should bring in a much bigger return on your investment in much quicker time. He's quite a catch, financially speaking. But he's a little old for you, don't you think?'

The insulting innuendoes behind Alex's suavely delivered speech brought her up with a jolt. Alex thought the same as Mario—that she was marrying Raymond for his money. Anger at such an offensive idea brought with it hot indignation, and some much needed common sense.

Alex was certainly right when he said he didn't love her any more, she conceded crossly. If he ever darn well did! He was probably declaring love for her seven years ago to justify what he'd done. He hadn't searched for her that hard, either. Maybe she *hadn't* left forwarding addresses but a determined pursuit would have found her. She hadn't actually been hiding.

No. Alex hadn't really loved her back then. Though perhaps he *had* felt some desire—she'd give him that. His lukewarm search had probably been inspired by an urge to take up where he'd left off that awful night. But then obviously one of those other women had come along and he'd forgotten all about her.

What right did he have to come here tonight and start looking down his nose at her choice of husband? How dared he judge her in such a demeaning fashion?

Raymond was worth ten of a man like Alex. Raymond would never be so cruel, or so hurtful, or so damned fickle! He was good and kind, strong and steady. He was like a rock. And that was what she wanted in her life. A rock, to rely on.

'No,' she said with cold firmness. 'I *don't* think Raymond's too old for me. And I don't appreciate your implication that I'm marrying him for his money.'

'Surely you're not going to tell me you're in love with him?'

The dry mockery in Alex's voice did what Judith's will-power could not achieve by itself. It totally doused any desire for the man she was dancing with.

'I'm not in the habit of agreeing to marry men I don't love,' she said frostily.

'Oh, really?'

This added innuendo did not escape her, either.

'Yes, *really*,' she countered caustically. 'I loved Simon too. With the sort of love that would have lasted and been the solid basis of a good marriage. What I felt for you was nothing but a passing and strictly mindless passion. I can see that now. As for your telling me that you were in love with me and that you searched fruitlessly for me, save it, Alex. If you'd really wanted to find me, you would have.'

She opened her mouth to reveal that she knew he'd come to Simon's house looking for vengeance, and to add that if he'd become entrapped by his own vile actions in a passion which he hadn't expected, then tough! But then she recalled her obligation to protect Karen and closed her mouth again.

'I think there are things about Simon you don't know,' he persisted ruefully. 'He wasn't worthy of any woman's love.'

Judith was angered that he should try to blacken Simon's name after all these years. It showed that his need for vengeance still overrode any supposed feelings he'd ever had for her. 'You're wrong on both counts,' she shot back. 'There were no secrets between Simon and me,' she improvised, protecting Karen while letting Alex know she knew about his sister's affair with Simon. 'He told me everything.'

'He would not have told you this,' Alex muttered. 'For if he had you would never have condoned such behaviour.'

'I know what you're referring to and, yes, I know about that as well. And it wasn't a matter of condoning, but understanding. Simon was no less of a sinner than any other man where sex was concerned. I'm sure you can appreciate how particularly difficult it can be for a man to control his desires when an attractive female throws herself at him.'

His laugh was full of scorn. 'She didn't throw herself at him! He went after her as he went after every female he fancied. With no mercy or respect. My God, I can't believe you knew! How could you have still been going to marry him, knowing what he was like?'

'What do you mean by that?'

'I mean he was a shameless bastard who loved nobody but himself.'

'Of course you would have to think that. It justifies what *you* did, doesn't it, in attempting to seduce me?'

'I won't deny there is some truth in what you're saying. I did feel Simon's vile behaviour justified my acting on what I felt for you. I didn't want to see you married to such a man. Obviously I didn't understand you already knew the nature of the beast, and were prepared to turn a blind eye to his decadence.'

'Oh, come now, Alexander. Decadence? That's exaggerating the situation, surely?'

He stopped dancing and simply stared down at her. 'I suppose I shouldn't be shocked. Anything goes these days when it comes to sex. Yet you seemed so innocent back then. So naïve. I see I made a big mistake. You weren't at all as you seemed.'

He clasped her back to him and resumed dancing, holding her closer than ever. 'So tell me, Judith,' he drawled, mockery back in his voice, 'what would have happened if Simon hadn't come along that night? Would you have gone ahead with the wedding anyway? Would you have let me stand there as best man next to your loving spouse while you went to bed with me on the side? Or was it just a oncer? A last sewing of your female oats, so to speak. What a pity Simon wasn't as understanding as you were, sweetheart. He didn't seem to understand *your* sinning one little bit!'

Outrage had her wrenching herself out of his arms, her mouth agape with anger. She was about to tear strips off him when she saw Margaret watching them from a distance, her long, scrawny neck stretched to the limit to see over the heads of the other couples who were, thankfully, providing Judith and Alex with some privacy from Margaret's spying.

'Think what you like,' she said curtly, and, placing her hands back in a formal dancing position, she urged Alex to move around the room.

'Oh, I will, Judith,' he said with silky menace. 'I will. I think it's particularly telling that when I find you a second time you're on the verge of marrying another very wealthy man whom you claim you love but whom I know you feel not one shred of passion for.'

Her eyes flew to his in sheer disbelief at the degree of cold ambition he attributed to her. 'What right have you to say a thing like that? You don't know any such thing.'

'Ah, but I do know, Judith,' he taunted softly. 'I know because after one minute's miserable dancing you wanted *me* again, dear heart.'

Her face flamed as much with shame as with indignation. For she could hardly deny what he was saying. She *had* wanted him.

'Not that I think your desire is exclusive to yours truly,' he went on with an oddly casual contempt. 'I saw the way you were letting that lounge lizard paw all over you earlier. Your brother-in-law-to-be, isn't he? How convenient. No doubt he's hoping to take up some of the slack in your sex life after you become Mrs Raymond Pascoll.'

Judith could not believe what she was hearing. 'I won't listen to any more of this.' And she went to leave.

But his hand shot out to grab her upper arm and yank her back into his arms before she could escape.

'Oh, yes, you will.' He laughed darkly as he steered her through the pulsing throng of people. Some of the couples were disco-dancing. Not Alex, however. He kept their bodies glued together, reviving once again the tempestuous feelings that only he could evoke in her.

'I've got seven years of questions bubbling up inside me, sweetheart,' he muttered, 'though I think I've finally worked out the reason behind that miserable letter you sent me after Simon's funeral. It was just an excuse, wasn't it? All that garbage about guilt. It wasn't guilt keeping you from me. It was my lack of money. I was too poor for you.'

Judith groaned. Things were going from bad to worse!

'But I'm not poor any more,' he whispered in her ear. 'I'm loaded. What a pity you didn't wait! You know, there was a time when it killed me to think you might be lying in another man's bed instead of mine. But that time has long past. I think it's going to give me real pleasure to think of you lying in Raymond's bed tonight. Especially now that I know you'd much prefer mine.'

He urged her over into a dimly lit corner where he reduced their dancing to nothing more than a blisteringly sensual swaying. The palm of his hand branded hers with its heat. His breath seared her hair. His body reared up hot and hard between them.

Judith was moments away from spontaneous combustion herself. Alex's mocking and misguided contempt was as nothing compared to the power of her perverse passion for him. It vibrated from her pounding heart, out into the far-reaching extremities of every jelly-like limb, obliterating everything she should be feeling. The strength of her desire had routed any indignation and had her clinging to him, showing him with her body language that she wanted him more than ever.

'Of course there *is* a way to remedy the situation, Judith, darling,' he murmured ever so softly, his smouldering palm moving seductively up her spine to where her dress ended and bare flesh began. 'Come with me right now. Tell Raymond you've changed your mind about marrying him. Tell him you've decided to marry me instead. I promise you, you won't lose out, either in bed or in your bank balance. Raymond's a pretty rich old geezer but I'm richer.

'As for the sex,' he murmured, moist lips brushing the top of her ear, 'we were magic together once, Judith. More than magic. It was like music. Not this kind of music. Nothing so low-key. When I kissed you that night, cymbals clashed. When I touched you, violins soared. Believe me when I say that when we finally do make love the drum beats will echo long into the night...'

Judith felt herself being inexorably drawn into the erotic web he was spinning. He was the spider and she was the fly, his words were the silk, his hands on her body her eternal damnation. Her lips were already parting to whisper his name, plus total surrender to his will, when, unexpectedly and abruptly, Alex straightened, putting a dampening distance between her throbbing body and his. His voice, when he spoke, was clipped and cold.

'Well, what do you say? Is it a yes or a no? How would you fancy being Mrs Alexander Fairchild?'

Her eyes were like saucers as they lifted to his. She saw the cold ruthlessness in his chilling black gaze, and a shiver of self-revulsion rippled down her spine. So close, she realised. So horribly, horribly close.

'You're mad!' she exclaimed on a raw rasping note.

And so was she. For there was a part of her…a very dark part, admittedly, but a part nevertheless…that was still tempted to say yes, to throw her pride and self-respect to the four winds, just so she could lie in his bed, even for one night.

'Not at all,' he denied with a casual shrug of his shoulders. 'Nowadays, I simply don't let things like my once far too active conscience get in my way. I go for what I want without fear or favour, and generally speaking I get it. Neither do I stupidly take what people tell me at face value. I close my ears to convincing liars and let the facts speak for themselves. And the facts tell me you're a deviously clever and very manipulative little fortune hunter, Judith.

'Yet I still want you, strange as it might seem. I don't love you, of course, but there again what's love got to do with the proposals *you've* accepted?'

'How dare you?'

'I take it that's a no? Too bad. I was hoping you weren't going to complicate the issues here. For you will be mine, Judith, one way or another.'

'I want you to leave,' she gasped, her heart thudding madly. 'I want you to...'

'I know exactly what you want me to do.' His laugh was truly wicked as he whirled her back into the middle of the dance-floor. 'You simply don't have the courage to say so. You're an emotional coward, Judith. You run away whenever your passionate heart threatens to overrule the plans that hard little head of yours has mapped out.

'But there's no running away this time. I'm here to stay, and I aim to use both your passion and your ruthless ambition to get what I want. Which is you and me, Judith, doing exactly what Simon stopped us from doing seven years ago.

'Now do stop scowling and smile sweetly at your current fiancé,' Alex suggested drily when the man in question came into sight, walking towards them with a slight frown on his face. 'Or do you want me to tell him what really happened seven years ago? I dare say it's a different version from the lily-white story *you* told. I'll bet you came out looking a truly tragic heroine.

'Come to think of it, the truth might change dear old Raymond's mind about marrying you, my sweet. That should uncomplicate the issues for you, not to mention the decisions. You'd have to choose between my very appealing offer, or eventually going back to work for a living. Fifty grand won't go far. I have a feeling that might increase my odds of success, don't you think?'

When Raymond's frown deepened on his approach, Judith dredged up a smile from somewhere, though she was seething inside with a hate which knew no bounds. 'If you say a word to Raymond,' she bit out through clenched teeth, 'I'll kill you.'

'No, you won't. Women like you don't kill. They lie and cheat and sleep around, but they don't kill. Raymond!' he said heartily when he was far too close for comfort. 'I must apologise for keeping your lovely Judith away for so long but she's such a good dancer, and it's been years since I danced with her. You didn't mind, did you?'

'No, no, of course not!' Raymond said with expansive *bonhomie*. 'I'm glad to see you two getting along so well. Shall we return to the others?' He took Judith's arm and the three of them began walking back towards the main living room.

'Was there any reason we shouldn't get along?' Alex said in a seemingly ingenuous manner. 'Judith, what ever have you been telling Raymond about me?'

'Nothing,' she said stiffly. 'I—'

'Come now, Judith,' Raymond broke in. 'There's no point in pretending. Better to clear the air once and for all, don't you think?'

They all stopped walking, with Judith trying to tell Raymond with her eyes to drop the subject. But he had never been one to take much notice of others, once he had his mind set on something.

'It's this way, Alexander. Judith mentioned you argued with her fiancé the night he was killed. Just before he drove off, in fact. She has felt all these years that you were partly to blame for the man's death. When she found out you were going to be here to-night, she didn't want to come. I told her she was being irrational and quite unfair to you. I explained how Simon sounded like he was the sort of man who could not hold his liquor well, and was obviously prone to driving while intoxicated.

'I thought I'd got through to her, but I wasn't sure till I saw you smiling at each other just then. I can't tell you how relieved I am. Judith's happiness is very important to me.'

'That's very commendable, Raymond,' he returned smoothly. 'But I must say I agree with Judith some-what. It has taken me many years to get over the feel-ing that I was to blame for what happened to Simon. Logic tells me he brought about his own demise by his recklessness, but the heart does not always respond to logic, does it?'

'Would you think me rude if I asked what you ar-gued about?' Raymond asked.

Judith swallowed when Alex swung his eyes her way. 'You didn't tell him?' he asked with mock in-nocence.

'I...I...' Her flustered stammering seemed to puzzle Raymond, and it irked her no end. She simply hated having to stand here in front of this black-hearted devil and let him play with her like this. Better that the truth should come out than that she should have to endure this torture.

But how could she tell Raymond the truth without

damaging everything—her relationship with him, plus his business dealings with Alexander?

Salvation came from the enemy himself.

'Judith never knew,' Alex lied, somewhat ironically, since it was what she'd told Raymond herself. 'But the fact is, it was about Judith herself. I didn't like the way Simon's family treated her.'

Judith blinked her surprise while Raymond looked very interested. 'Oh? In what way?'

'They made it clear they thought her...unsuitable to be the wife of the son and heir of the Frazier family's massive fortune.'

'Simon was a wealthy man, then? You never mentioned that, Judith.'

'He wasn't at that time,' she denied swiftly. 'He lived a simple life on the salary he earnt as a junior banking executive.'

'But he *was* due to come into a considerable amount of money upon his marriage,' Alex stated.

The news stunned Judith. It was the first she'd heard of such an inheritance. Alex frowned at her obvious shock.

'In that case, perhaps it's as well you never married the man, Judith,' Raymond said rather pompously. 'Nothing worse than one's family not approving of your wife.'

It was an ironic thing for him to say in the light of Margaret's obvious disapproval of her.

The woman herself materialised next to their threesome, her arm linked through Joyce's, who still looked rather down in the mouth. She hadn't been well, she'd told Judith earlier in the evening, and she didn't look well, either, her face pale and pinched.

'I've made coffee in the dining room,' Margaret said, 'for anyone who'd like some. Joyce here also brought along some of her prized chocolate peppermint slice for supper. Do you have a sweet tooth, Mr Fairchild?'

'I'm afraid not. But coffee sounds marvellous. Then I will have to call a taxi, Raymond. I'm an eight-hour-a-night boy from way back and I'll need a sharp mind about me tomorrow if I'm to get the better of the man I'm dealing with.'

Raymond chuckled and clapped him on the shoulder. 'Flattery won't get you a better price for that land of yours.'

'Neither will falling asleep on the job.'

'I can't imagine you doing that. Come. I'll show you the way to the dining room.'

Judith was taken aback when Raymond took Alexander's arm and walked off with him, leaving her behind. Margaret slanted her a sly smirk while Joyce managed to look almost sympathetic.

'I take it you don't want coffee?' Margaret said smarmily when Judith didn't move a muscle. She just stood there and stared after the departing men, her thoughts as chaotic as her emotions.

It was Joyce who tried to come to her rescue. 'Don't be upset,' she said with a sigh. 'He doesn't mean anything by it. Nothing is as important to Raymond as his business, you know.'

Margaret gave a short dry laugh. 'Judith's not upset by Raymond's behaviour, Joyce. She doesn't give a damn if Raymond ignores her. It's Mr Fairchild who's upset you, isn't it, Judith, dear? You've no idea the questions he plied me with earlier on. All about you. He just couldn't know enough. Care to tell us exactly what he once meant to you?'

Judith turned to face her future sister-in-law and saw naked hatred in Margaret's pale beady eyes. It sparked a most uncharacteristic defiance. There was no way she was going to let this mean-spirited witch destroy her relationship with Raymond. He might not be perfect but he was a good man, and she knew she could be happy with him, once Alexander was out of the picture. Just as she knew she could have been happy with Simon.

Physical passion was not the be-all and end-all. Look what it had done in the past, and what it had already done tonight. It had totally shattered her equilibrium, and her peace of mind; made her want what was essentially wrong for her.

Judith refused to give in to temptation a second time. She would not throw away a lifetime of potential happiness for the promise of passing pleasures. She would fight Alexander's wicked intentions as strongly as she would fight Margaret's. For both of them were selfish, and bitter about life. They were destroyers, and she wanted no more of destruction, least of all self-destruction.

No, Alexander could do his damnedest this time, she vowed valiantly, and he would not succeed. And neither would Margaret.

Judith stunned both of the women watching her by smiling the coolest and most confident smile. 'You think I don't know my Raymond by now?' she directed first at Joyce. 'I understand his priorities, and respect them. He has not upset me in the slightest.

'As for Mr Fairchild,' she went on, swinging her attention back to a sour-faced Margaret, 'he never meant anything to me, though I have to confess that I do not like the man. And, yes, his presence tonight has upset me. For Raymond's sake, I've tried to be polite. But it seems I'm not much of an actress if you've seen my true feelings shining through. Now I'm off to the dining room for coffee, where I'll see if I can do better.'

She whirled round and walked off but had only gone a few steps before Margaret joined her, sending words hissing with hatred across the space between them.

'Brave words, Judith. And bold. But you don't fool me. I watched you dancing with that man and I know, I tell you. You were lovers once and you're planning to be lovers again. You're going to cuckold my brother as surely as night follows day and I'm going to be there to catch you at it. And when I do I'm going to spit in your face!'

Judith ground to a halt, hot blood in her cheeks and hot words on her tongue-tip. But she never had a chance to deliver them. For they'd reached the doorway of the dining room and Raymond was waving them over, waving and smiling, oblivious of what was going on around him, oblivious of everything but entertaining an important business contact.

Alexander was standing by his side, a coffee-cup at his lips. His eyes over the rim found Judith's, but they were strangely unreadable. They went from Judith to Margaret then back to Judith, narrowing in the process. One of his eyebrows arched slightly as he drew the cup away from his mouth, giving Judith the impression he'd made some sort of surprising though satisfying observation.

His eyes locked with hers again, and this time she saw raw resolve in them.

'You will be mine…' he'd said. And his eyes seemed to be saying the same thing.

Even from that distance, Judith quivered beneath the force of their intent. She wondered if Margaret was witnessing the same, and jumping to the same conclusion.

'Do come in, ladies,' Alex said smoothly.

Judith wanted to flee then, away from him, away from everyone. And, in the light of what was to come, maybe she should have.

CHAPTER FIVE

ALEXANDER left straight after coffee, as he'd said he would, Raymond having called a taxi for him. A wave of relief flooded through Judith once he'd gone, though she did her best not to show anything in front of Margaret.

But she was afraid for the future. Raymond was to have ongoing business dealings with Alexander for a few days yet. He'd just asked him home for dinner the following night, doing so in front of his suspicious sister. What could Judith do but pretend it meant nothing to her, even though all the while her stomach had churned with a frantic fear?

Alex was not a man to forgive or forget, Karen had said. And he obviously imagined himself as some kind of wronged party in all this, which was perverse in the extreme, given the circumstances.

Still, it was too late to tell him about Karen's visit now. Far too late. It would achieve nothing. It might even make her look worse for not having confronted him with it at the time. He would simply conclude that she hadn't cared enough to do so. She would have betrayed Karen's confidence for nothing. Alex believed she was a cold-blooded gold-digger, marrying for money while she amused herself with other men on the side.

Indeed, he'd vowed to be *one* of those other men! No, not one, she amended in her chaotic mind. He wanted to be the *only* man in her bed. Alex was not the type to settle for sharing a woman. He was going to try to seduce her away from Raymond, to break up her engagement, then coerce her into some kind of cold sexual arrangement. Maybe marriage, and maybe not. Judith had no doubt his intention was to divorce or discard her, once he'd had his fill.

The man had become a sexual predator of the worst kind. And she, silly fool that she was, was his perfect victim. Everything was working against her. Her passion for him. Her lack of any strong desire for Raymond. Even her virginity.

She could not get the words he'd whispered to her on the dance-floor out of her mind. Those drum beats were pounding in her head, in her imagination. She could still feel the pulsating rhythm of his body and the stark outline of his arousal pressing into her, giving her a small taste of what it might feel like not just rubbing gently against her stomach but actually surging deep inside her.

Oh, dear heaven…

Suppressing a groan of despair, Judith valiantly plastered a plastic smile on her face and slid a brave but quivering arm through Raymond's. 'Shall we rejoin the other party-goers?' she asked him with false brightness. 'Or go home?' She was dying to escape Margaret's narrow-eyed gaze, dying to go home and unburden her worries to Peter Panda.

Raymond looked at his watch. 'It is getting rather late, and I have an early start in the morning. Alex is flying me down to have a first-hand look at the properties I'm interested in. I have to be at Mascot heliport by eight.'

'You're going by helicopter?'

'Yes. Alex's. He not only owns it but flies it as well. The man knows how to do things in style, I'll give him that. But he's wasting his time. I've already had a very thorough report and valuation of the three lots of land I've got my eye on, but Alex insists I see them for myself. I think he imagines I'll pay the ludicrous price he's asking with a bit of luxury and soft-soaping.

'But it'll take more than a fancy helicopter ride to sway Raymond Pascoll's business acumen,' he finished, his chest puffing up as his face adopted a pompous, supercilious expression.

Judith recoiled from this unaccustomed display of almost adolescent arrogance. She'd never associated Raymond with that type of male ego before, which she supposed was naïve of her. A man as successful as Raymond had to have an ego. What disturbed her was how childish he'd sounded. And there she'd been, earlier in the evening, thinking that he was the rock she would rely on, a man of maturity any woman would be proud to marry.

Judith's head whirled during the drive home. She felt as if she was on a never-ending roller-coaster ride, her thoughts going round and round, up and down.

It was all Alex's fault, she'd decided by the time the Mercedes slid smoothly into its garage. His sudden re-emergence into her life was confusing her, making her doubt herself and her feelings for Raymond. Before he'd arrived on the scene she'd been quite sure she was doing the right thing in marrying Raymond. His presence was even affecting Raymond, making him act differently, bringing out his competitive male side at its infantile worse.

You have to ignore Alex, the voice of desperation whispered in her head. Have to!

Judith shuddered as she climbed out of the car. She only had to remember what had happened earlier tonight on the dance-floor to appreciate the power he could exert if she gave him a single sexual inch. He would take more than a mile this time if she let him, and in doing so would destroy another fine man, along with everything she personally valued. Her self-respect. Her peace of mind. Her future. And any hope of happiness.

'Care for a nightcap?' Raymond asked on their way through the house towards the stairs.

Judith managed a sweet smile over her shoulder as she hurried on ahead across the foyer, anxious for the sanctuary of her bedroom. 'I don't think so. I'm very tired.'

'Too tired for a goodnight kiss?'

Judith stopped on the first step, swallowed, then turned, to find Raymond very close behind her. Long, lean fingers closed over her shoulders. Narrowed and very steely grey eyes met hers. His head was already dipping and all she could hear was a scream going through her head.

No, don't. I don't want you to kiss me. I don't want you to touch me. I don't want you!

She froze as determined lips covered hers, then gasped when those lips began prising hers open. His tongue snaked deep into her mouth and she almost gagged. He had never kissed her like this before. Never!

Judith wasn't sure if she was repulsed or simply shocked. Whatever, he obviously took her whimpering moan for encouragement, for she had to endure the astonishing demands of that marauding tongue for an interminable time before it finally withdrew, leaving her panting for breath.

'How in God's name are you still a virgin?' he rasped, releasing her shoulders to cup her flushed face. 'You know, I had no idea what a sexy woman I was engaged to till I saw you tonight in that dress. And I had no idea how much I wanted you till I saw you dancing cheek to cheek with another man...'

His thumb moved up to caress her left cheek and it took all of her control not to think of Alex, whose cheek it was which had rested there.

'If you weren't still a virgin, I'd take you to bed here and now,' Raymond proclaimed presumptuously. 'But the idea of you being untouched on our wedding night appeals to me. I wasn't too sure I liked your lack of experience when you first told me. It was rather...unnerving. But I can see you're a responsive girl. And not nearly as shy as I thought...'

His hands left her face to push the jacket back from her shoulders, his almost lascivious grey eyes dropping to her chest. 'You have the most beautiful breasts,' he said thickly, and cupped them with his hands.

Judith sucked in a sharp breath when his thumbs brushed over the still hard nipples, shocked by the electric charge which ricocheted through her. Yet she soon realised it wasn't Raymond's touch her body was responding to. Any touch would have brought some pleasure. Her body had been on red alert since the moment she knew she would see Alex tonight. Her breasts, and especially her nipples, had responded shamelessly to Alex during their dance together. Sexually, she'd been on fire since that moment, and that fire was clearly unabated.

But Raymond imagined her arousal was for him. And she let him think it, hoping in her despair and her desperation that one day it might be.

But it wasn't on this night, and in the end guilt crippled Judith's will to let him continue. It wasn't right, letting one man make love to you while you burnt for another.

'You...you must stop,' she groaned, pushing him away and dragging the jacket up over her shoulders and wrapping it tightly around her chest.

'You're right,' he muttered gruffly. 'I'm sorry. I was getting carried away.'

But I wasn't, Judith agonised. The longer he'd touched her, the less she'd liked it. Oh, God, what was she going to do?

'Go to bed, Judith,' he said brusquely, frustration in his flushed face.

'I...I'm so sorry,' she practically sobbed.

'You've done nothing to be sorry for.'

She almost said it then, almost told him she couldn't marry him. But instead she turned and ran up the stairs, along the hallway and into her room. She tried not to slam the door, lest Raymond should come after her, closing it quietly, then she leant against it with her heart thudding and her head pounding. Slowly, she became aware of all those beady black toy eyes looking at her, reproaching her.

'Yes, all right!' she burst out at last, levering herself away from the door. 'It was wrong of me. And wicked. But my intentions were good. I want to do the right thing by Raymond. I really do!

'But I don't know what the right thing is any more,' she wailed, lifting a shaking hand to her throat. 'I thought I could cope with a lukewarm sex life. I thought that would be preferable to those other crazed feelings Alex can evoke and which run rampant with my control and my conscience and lead to nothing but destruction. But, dear heaven, I'm not sure any more...'

She sank down on the edge of her bed and buried her face in her hands. But, astonishingly, no tears came. It was as though she was beyond tears, beyond anything which would give her comfort. She didn't even want Peter Panda.

A face loomed up in her mind, a handsome but harshly sculptured face with cold black eyes and a cruelly sensual mouth.

That's what you want, came the whisper of her darkest desires. Admit it!

Judith took her hands away from her face and straightened. She stared at her glittering blue eyes in her dressing-table mirror, at her parted lips and still panting chest.

'All right,' she bit out. 'I admit it. I want him. But I'm not going to act on that want. To do so would be really wicked, and I'm not that kind of person. I'm going to hold onto my standards and self-respect and soon Alex will go away.'

She hoped.

But what if he moved his business base to Sydney? What if he had no intention of really going away again, now that he knew where she lived? What if he wouldn't be satisfied till he'd shattered her life completely out of some kind of weird revenge for supposed wrongs?

Alex was good on revenge. He never forgot, or forgave. Karen had said so.

No, that was too over the top, she decided, trying to control her panic with logic.

'It's not as though he loves me,' she muttered as she stood up and started to undress. 'It's just a bruised ego thing. Or a temporary lust thing. Or whatever. He'll give up once he realises he's getting nowhere. Then, after he's gone, I'll see how I feel about Raymond. If it still doesn't feel right, I'll just have to break our engagement, I guess. That's the best I can do. But I'm not going to make a decision while Alex is on the horizon. He distorts my vision of things, and my judgement. I just know it!'

Judith hung the hateful yellow outfit in the back corner of the wardrobe, vowing it would never see the light of day again. She would never be able to look at it now without thinking of Alex. And she didn't want to do that any more than was necessary.

Already tomorrow night's dinner loomed as one horror after another in her mind. Maybe she could come up with a legitimate-sounding excuse this time for avoiding the encounter. Or maybe she would find the courage to face him one more time and convince him with an Oscar-winning performance that she didn't want him one little bit!

Yes, that was what she *had* to do. It was the only way to get him out of her life once and for all. She would treat him with cool politeness in Raymond's presence, but with the cold contempt he deserved if and when they were ever alone. It was a dangerous game but there again Alex was a dangerous man, blind to everyone's feelings but his own.

He claimed he no longer had a conscience. From what she could see, he was right about that. He did whatever he wanted to do these days without considering the consequences, or other people's feelings. Well, she would not let him ruin her life a second time. Nor Raymond's. Raymond didn't deserve that. Neither had Simon, for that matter, no matter what Alex told himself as an excuse.

Tears pricked as she thought of Simon.

Dear God, didn't Alex ever feel guilty any more over what they'd done? How could he dismiss what had happened without any real qualms, putting the blame on poor Simon? And how could he deliberately pursue her a second time, while she was engaged to another man?

It was like a ghastly repeat of the past. Or it could be, if she let it.

But she wasn't going to let it. She couldn't. It would be too much.

The tears began to flow then and she dived onto the bed, dragging Peter Panda into her arms and crying her heart out.

CHAPTER SIX

RAYMOND was gone by the time Judith went downstairs the next morning just after eight-thirty. Which she didn't mind. She hadn't wanted to explain her red-rimmed eyes.

She padded silently through the large empty house and into the equally large kitchen, surprised to find it too was empty. Mrs Cobb was usually there at this hour with a bright smile and some cheery gossip. A widow in her fifties, she had worked for the Pascoll family for yonks and was like part of the furniture.

Judith liked her and she liked Judith in return, though Judith wasn't sure if she approved of her marriage to Raymond. She'd asked her a couple of times if she was very sure she was doing the right thing, marrying a man so much older than herself.

Judith *had* been...till last night.

Sighing, she moved over to put on some water to boil for coffee. Propped up against the electric jug kettle was a note from Mrs Cobb saying she'd gone down to the supermarket and wouldn't be back till morning tea.

Pity, Judith thought. She could have done with some company, and distraction. Although on second thoughts perhaps it was better that the intuitive Mrs

Cobb wasn't there for a while. By the time she returned, her puffy eyes might be back to normal.

Breakfast was toast and coffee, which rather reflected her lack of any real appetite. It came to Judith as she sat at the breakfast bar absently sipping the coffee that she would have to go back to work soon. Even if she married Raymond, being a lady of leisure on a daily basis was not for her.

Admittedly, she had needed a complete break after the long job of nursing Mrs Pascoll. By the end, when she had been on twenty-four-hour call, she had been thoroughly exhausted. But now, after a few weeks of doing nothing, she felt ready to go back to nursing.

She needed to be busy. The devil, she appreciated with some irony, did indeed find work for idle hands.

She would also have to find something to do today, anything that would keep her mind off the coming evening with all its potential pitfalls. Judith knew cleaning was always a good antidote for thinking, so after breakfast she set about making Betty's job a darn sight easier by scrubbing all the tiles, floors and toilets in the four upstairs bathrooms, including the already spotless guest room *en suite*.

Betty was a nice girl who came in on Mondays and Fridays to do the heavier cleaning jobs in the huge twenty-room house. She had two small school-age children and a husband who didn't earn much, so she cleaned rich people's houses during the week to make ends meet. She often looked tired by Friday, and it would give Judith pleasure to give her an early mark tomorrow. She might even give her a little bonus of an extra fifty dollars. Send her off to get her hair done. Yes, she would do that.

Thinking of money reminded Judith of the fifty thousand dollars she'd been left in Maisie's will. Margaret had been furious. When she'd offered not to take it, Raymond had told her not to be so silly. She was to think of it as a bonus well earned and spend it on something special for herself. But Judith had still felt uneasy about accepting such a sum from an old lady who had been her patient. Margaret was right in so far as elderly people were often inclined to make ill-considered and generous gestures where their nurses were concerned.

It wasn't as though she needed the money. Judith had always been a saver and her bank balance was quite healthy.

In the end, she'd given the money to her mother to use as a down payment on a small flat not far from Helen's place. Helen was expecting her third baby, and her mother had often expressed the desire to have a little place of her own rather than live in the increasingly crowded council flat. Actually, the gift had been as much for Helen as her mother. Judith knew that Mrs Anderson was not an easy woman to live with. Still, she had been gratified at how delighted her mother had been.

Judith had been tempted to tell Alex all this the previous night but had known what his reaction would be. One of cynical derision. Why not give it away? There would be plenty more where that came from once she was Raymond's wife. She was damned if she did tell him, and damned if she didn't!

Still, if he started insulting her tonight, she was going to stand up for herself more. She'd been so taken aback by the turn of events the previous evening that she hadn't defended herself as well as she would have liked. The man only had to come within twenty feet of her and all rational thought flew out of the window. She would have to have her wits about her tonight, that was for sure.

Sighing, Judith moved on to the downstairs powder room, scrubbing and rubbing till everything shone.

'Anyone would think you were eight and a half months pregnant,' Mrs Cobb commented when she finally stopped cleaning for afternoon tea.

Judith's puzzled expression brought a laugh from the jolly-natured housekeeper.

'When I was expecting both my boys,' she explained, 'I got so wrought up with nerves during the last couple of weeks, I started washing walls and windows to get my mind off what was to come. I didn't stop till I went into labour.'

Her happy smile suddenly faded and her look was sharp. 'Are you worried about something, love? Can I help, perhaps?'

The temptation to confide in Mrs Cobb was intense, but Judith was worried that voicing her concerns to the well-meaning woman might actually make them worse. Especially with Alex coming for dinner tonight. Her only protection against him, Judith realised, was a superbly crafted façade. How could she sit there at the dining table looking cool and composed while Mrs

Cobb served the meal, knowing the housekeeper knew her deep, dark secret?

No, it was better to keep this wicked weakness to herself. Besides, a lady of Mrs Cobb's generation might be absolutely disgusted at Judith's feeling anything like the wildly rampant and totally irrational desire which swamped her whenever she even thought of Alex. Judith found it pretty disgusting herself in the cold light of day.

She could almost excuse her behaviour seven years ago, when she'd been young and naïve and hadn't known any better. And when she had been able to delude herself into thinking she was in love.

But now she knew the awful truth. Her feelings—and Alex's too—had nothing to do with love and everything to do with sheer animal lust. It was a primitive and primal force which had to be kept in check and on a very firm leash. Let it off for even a second and it would run rampant, as it had last time, with disastrous consequences.

Judith shuddered at this knowledge, plus the danger of being in Alex's presence again, especially considering his ugly vow to seduce her through fair means or foul. The only way she would survive would be to close ranks around herself, to conceal her inner frailty behind a steel shell of bitter resolve.

Keep thinking of Simon, she told herself staunchly. Then Raymond. Do you want to leave another shattered man behind? Maybe not his body but certainly his spirit and self-esteem. Raymond might not be madly in love with you but he does care about you. He even desires you now. Dear God, do you want

Margaret to be right about you? Are you that weak and wicked?

Judith could not bear to think of any of those things happening. Thoughts of another night of shame fuelled her determination to remain strong in the face of even the most cleverly devised temptations. Alex could offer her the world and she would not surrender. Never!

'Is it your marriage to Mr Pascoll?' Mrs Cobb prompted. 'Are you having second thoughts about it?'

'Good heavens, no,' she returned brightly while she willed any guilt from showing in her face. 'I'm just bored, that's all. There are only so many books you can read and so many videos you can watch. I need to get back to work. To nursing. It's what I do well, and what makes me feel worthwhile.'

Which was true. In a way, she was lost without her nursing. It was what she'd always wanted to do, right from when she'd been a little girl.

Mrs Cobb nodded as she dunked her biscuit in her tea. 'I know what you mean. I always think I'd like to retire and do nothing but I know I'd be climbing the walls in no time. Still, does Mr Pascoll know of your intention to go back to work after you're married?'

Judith blinked her surprise at the question, and the slightly worried tone behind it. This was something she hadn't discussed with him. She'd just assumed he understood that she would want to work, like most women these days.

'Are you saying he won't like me working?' she asked, frowning.

Mrs Cobb shrugged. 'I don't really know, but he's

an old-fashioned man. Perhaps you should ask him about it. *Before* the wedding,' she added drily.

Judith dragged in a deep breath, then let it out slowly. It was just over two weeks away now. Their wedding day. And a wedding day was inevitably followed by a wedding night…

She thought of Raymond's tongue in her mouth and his hands on her breasts, and a little shudder raced through her. Could she go through with this? Could she really?

Mrs Cobb's eyes on her were as watchful as Margaret's, though much more kind. 'It's not too late to change your mind, you know, love. It's never too late to change your mind, right up to the last minute.'

'Yes, I know that,' she returned, fearing her face must be showing a degree of distress. With a supreme effort of will she wiped her face clean of emotion and found a soothing smile. 'I'm fine. Truly. Margaret was a bit of a pain in the neck last night as usual, that's all. You know what she's like.'

'Oh, yes. Only too well. She's not a happy person, that one. And she's jealous of you, Judith.'

'She doesn't like me, that's for sure. Thank God she left home to marry Mario. I just hope Raymond doesn't expect us to socialise with them too much. Speaking of socialising, did Raymond say what time he'd be here with his guest tonight?'

'He said to expect them about seven. Dinner is for eight. You know how he likes to unwind with a few drinks beforehand.'

'Yes, I do. Look, I'll look after the drinks, *and* the fire. I'm sure you have enough to do with the dinner.

What did he order this time? Not that I can't guess. Home-made pumpkin soup, roast pork and...let's see...lemon meringue pie?'

'Right in one. You know Mr Pascoll very well, don't you? And I have to admit you both get along very well too. Just don't be too accommodating with him, Judith. Don't go along with everything he wants just to keep the peace.'

Judith was startled. 'Do I do that?'

'I don't think you're aware of it, but yes, you do.' Mrs Cobb settled a firm look upon her. 'You're a good girl, and a sweet one. It's not in you to argue back or to be aggressive, like some of these modern girls. But Raymond will walk all over you if you act the doormat with him. Just look at the way he's treated poor Joyce.'

Judith was really taken aback by that last statement. 'But what do you mean? How does he treat Joyce? I thought they had an excellent boss/secretary relationship.'

The housekeeper gave her the oddest look. It was almost pitying. She opened her mouth to say something, then closed it again, muttering something under her breath.

'I shouldn't be gossiping about my employer,' she said at last. 'Mr Pascoll's been very good to me and he's basically a decent man. But he isn't over-blessed with sensitivity, if you know what I mean.'

Judith nodded her agreement, sighing. 'I do know what you mean. And I will certainly keep what you've said in mind. Now I'd better go and start getting ready for dinner. I look a mess.'

Judith thought about what Mrs Cobb had said as she made her way slowly back up to her room. Did she always take the easy path when dealing with people, simply to avoid an argument or confrontation? Put her head in the sand, so to speak, lest someone take a swipe at it?

Maybe she had in the past but she hadn't last night, either with Raymond or Alex. Yet Alex had called her a coward...

Judith frowned. Cowards were weak people, afraid to face life and life's problems, always running away.

And wasn't that what she'd done after Simon's death? Run away? First to this house and now into a loveless marriage, because she was afraid of the alternative, afraid to face the person Alex could turn her into, afraid of passion.

No, no, she denied frantically. That wasn't how it was! She'd been understandably crippled by guilt and shame seven years ago. A man had lost his life because of what she'd done. An innocent man. It wasn't a matter of running away. It was a matter of survival. And common sense. And pride, damn it!

She could never have been happy with Alex back then, even if he hadn't just used her for revenge, even if he'd wanted her for more than a night or two. To seek that future for herself would have been both foolish and self-destructive. She'd chosen a more sensible, decent path. If it was a more secure and peaceful path too, then was that so wrong?

Her chin lifted defiantly as she mounted the staircase. No. She was doing the right thing in rejecting

Alex and all he represented and staying with Raymond.

Judith chose her clothes carefully, balancing common sense with a need not to arouse any suspicion in Alex that she was being falsely modest in his presence. After last night's provocative outfit, she could hardly go back to some of her more conservative dresses without him raising a cynical eyebrow.

So she chose what women always chose when their backs were to the wall. A little black dress.

It wasn't one of her recent purchases. She'd bought it a couple of years back in a sale because it was one of those dresses which would take her anywhere, made of stretch jersey wool and simple in style, with long straight sleeves, a fairly short skirt but a high neckline with a rolled collar. Yet strangely enough she'd only worn it once, when Raymond had taken her to the ballet.

Now it was making a second appearance, and for some reason it looked different. Slinkier somehow. And tighter.

Judith scowled at herself in the mirror. She must have put on a few pounds over the last few weeks on account of her idle lifestyle. Either that or she was just more aware of her body, encased as it was from neck to knee in the figure-hugging black material.

Her cheeks flushed at that last observation, for it was just the sort of awareness that Alex effortlessly evoked in her. Yet he wasn't even here! His arrival was still at least an hour away.

She went about finishing her dressing with a sense of despair, fearing that no matter what she did or what she wore the end result would be the same. Alex would take one look at her and know what she was feeling, and what she was secretly wanting.

Her hairdo would not fool him, irrespective of how severely she scraped it back from her face, or how plain the black clip was which clamped the abundant chestnut waves demurely at the nape of her neck.

Her lack of make-up would not fool him either, for already her cheeks were blushed with an unbidden excitement, her lips swollen as though eagerly awaiting a lover's kisses. The more she'd licked and bit their quickly drying surfaces in nervous agitation while dressing, the redder and more sensitive they had become.

Judith shook her head at herself in the mirror as she clipped elegant pearls to her lobes. It's just your guilty conscience, she kept telling herself. Keep your cool in his presence and Alex won't see a thing except a mature woman dressed in sophisticated black and pearls. He'll take your high colour for make-up. All you have to do is stay calm.

They arrived at seven-twenty, Raymond choosing to park his car out front and bring Alex through the front door, rather than through the garages. Judith had been waiting for them in the drawing room, an assortment of drinks at the ready, the red wine for dinner already breathing, the whites chilling in ice-buckets.

She'd already had a couple of sherries herself to steady her nerves, and when she saw the car lights swing into the driveway she rose from where she'd been sitting in front of the fire, instinctively knowing how Raymond would choose to make his entrance with a business colleague he wanted to impress.

Smoothing the skirt down over her hips, she squared her shoulders then walked with coolly elegant strides towards the front door. Raymond opened it before she could get there, ushering his guest in ahead of him.

Alex was wearing a pair of casual cream trousers, a toffee-coloured crew-necked sweater and a brown suede jacket with stitched pockets. The country-and-western-style outfit suited his tough macho looks and made Raymond, in his nondescript grey business suit, look anaemic by comparison.

Alex rubbed his hands together as he watched her approach, though not in gleeful anticipation, Judith realised after a moment's fright, but with cold. It was bitter outside, a cold snap down south having brought chill winds to Sydney.

'It's freezing out there,' he said, and blew on the tips of his fingers. 'Hello, Judith. You're looking nicely warm.'

'I've been sitting in front of the fire,' she explained coolly before bestowing a dazzling smile on Raymond. 'Hello, darling.' She kissed him on the cheek, standing between the two men to hide Raymond's look of astonishment. She'd never called him 'darling' before. It had been 'Mr Pascoll' for three years before it had finally become 'Raymond'. Judith was not a 'darling' sort of person.

'Did you have a good day?' she went on warmly. 'I've got the fire burning and all the drinks ready.' She linked arms with him and snuggled into his side, not giving Alex a second glance as she turned.

'I had a *very* good day,' Raymond returned, preening himself visibly at the adoring-little-woman treatment she was dishing out. He even bent to kiss her back on the cheek. 'And you're looking lovely, my dear. Have I seen that dress before?'

Judith's laugh was tinkling. 'This old thing? Of course you have, darling. I wore it when we went to the ballet one night.'

'Did you? Well, I like it. You should wear it more often. Now, I think we'd better get our friend here in front of the fire before he dies of terminal frostbite. He's been complaining of the cold all day.'

Judith glimpsed a chillingly cynical gleam in Alex's black eyes when she was finally forced to look his way again. He hadn't been fooled by her performance so far, it seemed.

'You're a lucky man, Raymond,' he drawled as he accompanied them into the plush warmth of the room. 'If I had this to come home to every night, I doubt I'd ever venture outdoors.'

Raymond chuckled appreciatively. 'Take a seat, Alex, while I pour you a drink.' He moved over to the huge antique sideboard which served as his bar. 'What would you like? And what about you, Judith? Your usual?'

'Not this time, Raymond,' she demurred. She'd already had enough sherry and knew he would expect her to sample some of the wines with her meal. Just enough alcohol sharpened her senses and gave her some much needed Dutch courage. Too much would leave her maudlin and depressed.

'I'll have a brandy, thanks, Raymond,' Alex said

smoothly as he settled himself into the armchair nearest the fire and directly across from the one Judith was occupying. Two empty chairs separated them, but nothing could come between their gazes. Every time Judith looked up from the fire it was to find coldly cynical black eyes upon her.

Without her realising it, her body language became tellingly tense in the minute it took for Raymond to join them. Her hands unconsciously gripped her chair's carved wooden armrests, her knees were pressed primly together, and her back was straight and stiff. Her relieved sigh when Raymond finally handed Alex his brandy and sank into the chair next to his guest with his own Scotch on the rocks brought a glance from her fiancé.

'Tired, my love?' he asked with far more solicitousness than usual.

'Just a little,' she said. 'I did some early spring-cleaning today.'

'But surely the cleaner can do that?' he retorted, his expression disapproving. 'That's what I pay her for!'

'I don't mind physical work, Raymond. I have to do something during the day. Actually, I've been thinking of going back to work.'

'Good God, why? Most of the wives of the men I know don't do a damned thing during the day except go to lunches and have their hair done. You're not married, are you, Alex?' he directed to his immediate right. 'Tell me, if you were, would you let your wife work? If you were married to a woman as beautiful and desirable as Judith, would you want her coming home at the end of the day exhausted and irritable from looking after sick people?'

'Absolutely not,' he murmured between sips of his drink, that merciless black gaze holding hers over the rim of the balloon glass.

Judith swallowed, then looked away into the dancing flames. She could hardly believe this conversation. Raymond was acting as if he looked upon marriage to her as the acquiring of an attractive and always available sexual possession. That was not the sort of marriage she'd envisaged when he'd proposed. She'd imagined a relationship based on friendship and companionship, a partnership based on mutual affection and respect. Sex was not to have figured largely in the picture at all!

The sound of the telephone ringing out in the hallway only just filtered through the heavy door.

'Mrs Cobb can get it,' Raymond pronounced when Judith went to get up.

Resentment bubbled up inside her as she reluctantly lowered herself back into the chair. Seconds later there was a tap on the door and Mrs Cobb popped her head in, announcing that there was a call for Mr Pascoll from his sister.

Raymond sighed and rose. 'I'll try not to be too long.'

A fraught silence fell upon the room once Raymond had closed the door on his way out. At least, it was fraught on Judith's side.

'If you were married to me,' Alex drawled into the thickened atmosphere, 'you'd be too exhausted to go to work in the first place.'

Judith only just managed not to react as he no doubt expected her to. With anger. She turned her head coolly to look at him, grateful that he wasn't able to hear her rapidly beating heart.

'I do not wish to engage in conversation with you while my fiancé is out of the room,' she said curtly.

'That's fine by me. You can just listen. I've had time to think about my reactions to your unexpected reappearance in my life last night, not to mention the rather impulsive things I said, and I find I regret them.'

Judith's eyes widened. Was an apology coming?

'After spending the day with your fiancé, I do not wish to pursue the subject of the past—or you—any further. Please accept my heartfelt apologies for any distress I might have caused you. Your secrets are safe with me, dear heart. I won't betray you to your beloved. Believe it or not, I find I quite like the fool. A bit pompous, but then we all have our faults. Though some faults are more insidiously attractive than others,' he added, his eyes dropping from her mouth to her breasts.

Judith blinked her shock. Never had such an insulting apology been made to her.

'I dare say you'll be quite happy together,' he resumed, his eyes lifting to her face again. 'Fortunately, Raymond doesn't have the insight or sensitivity to see that his little wife will always be faking it in the cot, not to mention elsewhere. That display of devotion at the front door was quite impressive. Rather a different tack from the one you used with Simon. You played the naïve little *ingénue* to perfection back then.

'Unfortunately, you haven't changed in other respects. I have no doubt you are going to be as faithless a wife to him as you would have been to Simon. Not that that would have worried Simon. But our Raymond is one of the old school when it comes to morals and he does seem to be genuine in his affection for you, so it won't be *me* who shatters his illusion that you care about him in return. I'll leave that to the Marios of this world.'

Judith burst from her chair, her colour as high as her agitation. She stood with her back to the fire, her arms crossed defensively in front of her as she glared down at him in pained outrage.

'How dare you say such things to me?' she cried, her voice shaking as much as her body. 'You have no right. No evidence! I...I'm not at all what you think. I wouldn't touch Mario with a bargepole. You have no idea how wrong you are about me.'

'Oh? And in what way am I wrong?' he said, peering up at her over the rim of his glass as he casually sipped and spoke at the same time. 'Do tell me, Judith. Wasn't that you seven years ago on the ground in Simon's garden, two days before your wedding, letting me do whatever I liked? Wasn't that you last night melting into me on the dance-floor as though you couldn't wait for a repeat performance?'

'Stop it,' she groaned, her hands reaching up to cover her burning cheeks.

Slowly, he lowered the brandy balloon into his lap and leant forward slightly, his eyes never leaving hers.

'Tell me that desire isn't crawling along your veins at this moment,' he whispered in a low, wickedly seductive voice. 'That you don't want me to kiss you, caress you, make love to you now...here in this room...on this floor...in front of this fire. Tell me you don't want me, Judith. Tell me...'

Fury burst through the fierce frustration that his words had managed to fire within her. 'I don't want you, damn you,' she flung at him, her hands balling into fists as they rammed down to her sides.

He settled back into his chair, the dark tension in his face smoothing into an expression of bored derision. 'Of course you're quite right. It isn't particularly me you want. Any attractive man would do. You must be very frustrated, having spent so much time landing this particular fish. I dare say you couldn't afford to be too blatantly unfaithful till you had Raymond secure, hook, line and sinker.

'Seven years, you said? What took you so long? I would have thought a man of Raymond's ego and age wouldn't be able to wait to claim that delicious body of yours as his own. Not that you wouldn't have been giving him some delectable little samples along the way. Was it you, perhaps, who delayed things? Were you waiting till the mother died and you saw if it was necessary to go the whole way into marriage?'

'You think you know it all, don't you?' she countered heatedly. 'But you know nothing, I tell you. If I use my supposedly delicious body to ensnare wealthy bridegrooms while sleeping around on the side, then how come I'm still a virgin? Tell me *that*, Mr Know-it-all!'

CHAPTER SEVEN

ALEX just stared at her, disbelief warring with shock on his face. He opened his mouth to say something but the door opening silenced him from voicing what was on his mind.

For her part, Judith was shaking inside. Why had she risen to his bait? And why had she made such a disastrous confession? What could she have hoped to achieve by it? He wouldn't believe her. He didn't believe a word she said! There was only one way to prove to him that she was a virgin and maybe even that would fail. A twenty-nine-year-old modern girl wasn't likely to have much physical evidence of virginity.

And why, in heaven's name, was she even *thinking* of proving her point that way? The man clearly despised her. Any feelings he might have once held for her had long since turned to a cynical contempt. It was all hopeless, utterly hopeless!

Her head whirling, she bent down to stoke the fire as Raymond stalked back into the room. By the time she rose from her haunches and turned around with seeming composure, Alex was sitting up straight in his chair, his brandy glass back at his lips. His eyes upon Judith were dark and thoughtful, bringing the small hope that she might have put a dent in his vile presumptions about her.

'Truly, that woman is an interfering fool!' Raymond exclaimed irritably as he resettled himself in his chair, his near-empty glass still in his hand. 'I think you were right about her last night, Judith. She can be very trying. But enough of Margaret,' he said as he downed the remainder of his whisky. 'I'm in too good a mood to spoil it with relative talk. Get me another whisky, would you, Judith?' he ordered, and handed her the empty glass.

She was glad to have something to do, though Mrs Cobb's warning about being a doormat to Raymond did slip into her mind. Still, the drink was easy to prepare. Half a dozen ice cubes over which she poured straight Chevas Regal. Raymond liked fine things and money was no object.

'Did Alex tell you we've sealed the deal about the land?' he asked when she handed him back the glass. With no thank-you, she also observed, irritation flaring.

'No,' came her brusque reply.

Raymond didn't seem to notice her change of mood. But Alex did, his brows lifting before drawing together in a frown. More and more Judith got the feeling that he was looking upon her differently now, that he wasn't so sure she was the wicked, fortune-hunting adventuress he'd believed her to be.

'I've already signed on the dotted line,' Raymond pronounced pompously. 'And we finally compromised on the price. I paid Alex more than *I* wanted to, and he accepted less than *he* wanted to.'

'So your business together is finished, then?' she asked, hating herself for the suddenly ambivalent feelings which were coursing through her. A minute or two ago she would have been relieved. Now she wasn't sure she wanted Alex to go, not while there was the beginnings of a slim hope that he might have started to believe her.

'Yes. Alex is returning to the South Coast tomorrow,' Raymond confirmed, and Judith's heart sank. 'I've told him he'd be better off based in Sydney but he doesn't agree. He says Sydney's too tough a town for him, which is a joke. Your friend is as tough as teak, Judith. I could have sworn no one could talk me into paying more for that land.'

'Don't flatter me, Raymond,' Alex joined in. 'I only had to point out some of the advantages which your reports didn't mention and you were wise enough to see the added value. The nearby railway line was the most important aspect, of course, especially with the price of road transport. The railways are running at such a loss these days they're eager to give the most incredible deals for cargo transport. You won't lose buying that land. All you need now are some good farmers to grow your crops.'

'Something you probably know more about then me as well, Alex. Judith tells me you were once a farmer.'

'Not willingly, and never again. My sister's husband took over my responsibilities there several years ago, thank the Lord, enabling me to seek wider horizons.'

'Karen's married?' Judith said before she could snatch the words back.

Alex looked up at her, a cloud passing over his eyes

as though he knew there was something wrong with what she'd said, but he wasn't sure exactly what. Yet.

'Yes, she is,' he told her. 'And she has two little boys, and a girl.' He cocked his head slightly on one side in an inquisitive gesture, that incisive mind of his ticking over. 'I didn't know you knew I had a sister named Karen, Judith.'

'Simon told me about her, remember?' was all she could think of to say. 'I...um...I mentioned it to you last night.' Thank heaven. At the time Alex hadn't been too pleased, thinking she'd condoned Simon's seducing innocent young girls. He'd jumped to the conclusion there and then that she was some kind of sexual swinger, obviously planning on having an open marriage with Simon. She wondered what he thought now, knowing she hadn't slept with Simon herself. *If* he believed her, that was.

'But I thought...' he began, then stopped, a frown, then a grimace sweeping across his face.

'Thought what?' she asked.

He reached up to comb his hair back from his face with his fingers and she noticed a sheen of perspiration on his forehead.

'Nothing,' he muttered. 'Do you mind if I take my jacket off? I'm beginning to feel a little warm.'

'Go ahead, but it's not as warm as this in the dining room,' Raymond warned. 'I'll just pop along and see if Mrs Cobb is ready to serve.'

Judith sat there, dry-mouthed, while Alex stood up and took off his jacket. The last thing she needed at that moment was a reminder of how well built the man was. Tomorrow, he would exit from her life again, never to return, and she would go on to marry Raymond. It was crazy of her to even think that anything at this stage would change that, crazy to imagine that they would suddenly declare their mutual love and everything would be all right.

Alex had already stated quite clearly that he didn't love her. As for her own feelings for him...

Love was not what she felt when she looked at him, she kept reminding herself. Not what she'd felt that night in Simon's garden. Nor what she'd felt when she was in his arms last night.

It was sex.

Grow up, Judith, the voice of common sense urged. Grow up and just let the man go. He's bad news.

'Talk to me, Judith,' he said impatiently from where he'd stayed standing in front of the fire.

She sighed an almost weary sigh and kept her eyes averted from him. 'What is there left to say between us?'

'I don't know,' he muttered. 'I just don't know.'

'You said everything that could be said a while back.'

'Maybe I was wrong.'

'Maybe you were.' Anger over his earlier assumptions put a twist of lemon on her tongue. 'You said you only believed in facts, Alex. Well, the fact is I was a virgin when I met you. And I'm still a virgin. How does that equate with what you believe me to be?'

'Actually, it equates quite easily, Judith, now that I come to think about it.'

Shock jerked her eyes up to his. They were hard

again, and quite cold. Where had his earlier doubts flown to, the beginnings of belief? Had she misinterpreted his body language?

'I've heard of women like you,' he elaborated. 'They're called bankers. They save up their virginity for just the right investment, capitalising on it for all its sometimes considerable worth. I can see that Simon would have found a virgin bride quite irresistible, provided she turned a blind eye at the right times. As for dear old Raymond, I imagine he might find an inexperienced wife quite a comfort. I can't imagine he'd want too many comparisons in the sack.'

Judith could only shake her head. Was there no end to his incredible conclusions about her? What was it that fuelled such a bitter scepticism in him that he had to invent an even worse scenario to fit the facts even as they changed?

'But where do I fit into all this, I ask myself?' he went on ruefully. 'Was I your one Achilles heel? Did you really lose all control that night as you seemed to? Or were you already used to dealing with your own frustrated desires in the most inventive ways, gaining satisfaction while still technically remaining a virgin?'

'You're sick, do you know that?' She stood up and went to leave, but he grabbed her wrist in an iron grip and whirled her back to face him.

'Actually, you're quite right,' he growled. 'I *am* sick. Have been all day. But I'm hiding it well, don't you think? I should be back in that hotel room, tucked up with a hot-water bottle and a couple of aspirin, but I had to come tonight. I had to see you again. How's that for being really sick? I told myself I would have none of you any more but I find I just can't do that, God help me.'

He groaned and grabbed her shoulder, yanking her hard against his heaving chest. 'I want you, Judith,' he rasped, 'and I will give anything to have you. If you break your engagement to Raymond and come with me now, tonight, I'll put five million dollars in your bank account tomorrow morning. Yes, that's how rich I am,' he added when her eyes widened. 'Just think of it. Five million dollars. What more could a girl like you want?'

What more indeed...?

Tears pricked at Judith's eyes. Tears of hurt, and tears of shame.

For once again she was tempted, as he'd always been able to tempt her. Not by the money, but by the man, and the devil which had temporarily taken possession of his soul. But this time the devil would not win.

She blinked away the tears and set a steely face upon him. 'You still have it all wrong, Alex,' she said. 'What kept me away from you seven years ago wasn't money but shame. What attracted me to Raymond wasn't money but decency. You know nothing of either any more. I feel sorry for you. I really do.'

But she felt sorrier for herself. She was obsessed with the man, and that obsession would not leave her after he was gone. It would remain to poison her relationship with Raymond, and her future happiness.

The realisation came to her then that she could not go through with this marriage. It wasn't fair to

Raymond. He deserved better than a wife whose heart and mind belonged to someone else, however perverse that possession might be.

She would tell him tomorrow. Or maybe the day after. As soon as she could muster the courage...

Dinner was a nightmare, full of awkwardly blank moments and inane replies to questions she hadn't heard. Her wine remained largely undrunk, though she ate the food. Mindlessly. Mechanically.

Alex tried to catch her eye a few times but she steadfastly refused to look at him. Her expression of pity earlier had clearly disturbed him, maybe even brought back some doubts about her. But she could no longer risk any contact with him, even visual. He was far too dangerous and warped a creature. And she was far too weak where he was concerned.

Still, it was a strain not to give in to the urge to look at him, which was what he obviously wanted, and by the time port was served back in the drawing room in front of the now smouldering fire Judith was running on empty.

'You look like you could do with a good night's sleep,' Raymond said, and Judith's head jolted upright from where it had sunk while she'd stared blankly into the almost hypnotic red embers.

It was with a degree of shock that she realised Raymond was talking to Alex. She glanced over at that harshly featured face and saw for the first time that what Alex had said earlier was true. He *was* sick.

Dark rings haunted his eyes and his cheeks were sunken with fatigue. Beads of perspiration covered his

forehead and his cheekbones held an unhealthy flush.
Since Alex had long since taken off his suede jacket
it didn't seem likely that he could be hot. The fire had
died down and the room was only pleasantly warm.

'Actually, I do feel a bit under the weather,' he admitted in that understated way men talked to each
other. It was clear to Judith's experienced and now
observant eye that he was quite ill.

Her natural tendency to sympathy surfaced, but she
managed to squash it down. He didn't deserve sympathy. The man had become corrupt over the years,
thinking his money could buy him anything he
wanted. Where once he might have been capable of
love, now he only felt lust. He'd become a cold-
hearted, ruthless predator and didn't need anyone feeling pity for him. If he was sick, then too bad. He
deserved worse.

'Could be flu coming on,' Raymond ventured.
'There are a lot of nasty strains going round this year.
I hear when they hit they can hit quite quickly. What
do you think, Judith? You're the nurse.'

'I think Alex should get home to bed straight away.'

'Good advice,' Raymond concurred. 'I'll call you a
cab.'

'I think I might go up to bed myself.' Judith stood
up, determined not to be left alone with Alex again.
'I'll say goodnight, Alex,' she managed, though tone-
lessly. 'It's been nice seeing you again.' Even if you
have destroyed my happiness a second time, she added
silently. Even if I'll never forget you now.

'Goodbye, Judith,' he returned. 'And good luck.'

The surprising sincerity in his voice startled her into

looking him in the face, and what she saw there made her heart contract. For a bitter remorse filled his eyes. He knew he'd really blown it with her, and he regretted it. What exactly he regretted she could not tell. Maybe only that he would never have the pleasure of taking that virginity he so scorned. Judith could not be sure. She certainly could not afford to start thinking he regretted misjudging her. On imagining he still loved her. That was the road to hell!

She turned and walked quickly towards the stairs and the sanctuary of her room.

Ten minutes later, she was lying on top of her bed, hugging Peter Panda and desperately holding back the urge to weep copious tears of self-pity, when Raymond's shout reached her. Startled, she put her companion down and hurried out into the hallway.

'Judith!' Raymond's voice shouted again from downstairs.

'Coming!' she called back, and broke into a run. Good God, what had happened? He sounded in a right panic.

The sight at the bottom of the stairs stunned her. Alex was down on his knees on the first step, his arms wrapped around the carved pole of the balustrade. Her shocked gasp seemed to snap his head up, like a puppet on a string. He just looked at her for a moment, before collapsing in a crumpled heap, his arms releasing their stranglehold so that he tumbled off the step onto the marble foyer with an almighty thump, banging his head loudly on the floor.

Raymond swore while Judith flew down the stairs, her heart racing with automatic concern. 'What happened?' she asked as she bent to check the back of his head then take Alex's pulse. There was no lump but his heartbeat was a little erratic.

'By the time the cab came, he'd started shivering and shaking quite violently. It was obvious he was very ill, so I told him not to go but to stay here where you could look after him.'

Judith's face must have shown her shock.

'Look, I know you don't care for him much, but you *are* a nurse, Judith,' Raymond said sternly. 'I couldn't very well let him leave to lie ill and alone in a hotel room, could I?'

Her sigh was resigned. 'No, I suppose not.'

'I started taking him upstairs and he just collapsed all of a sudden. Gave me one heck of a fright. I tried to pick him up but he's as heavy as lead. I'll have to get Mrs Cobb to help us carry him upstairs. Then I'll ring Harry.'

Harry was Dr Larson, who'd been Maisie's GP, chosen because he was the only local one who would make house calls. Still, he was a fair enough doctor, and very conscientious—something which was worth its weight in gold.

'He might be able to walk with our help in a minute,' she said. 'I think he might have fainted. Look, he's coming around.'

'Wh—what h-h-happened?' he asked, his voice shaking along with his body.

'You collapsed on the stairs, and then you fainted,' Judith supplied tersely. 'Now, do you think you can get upstairs with our help?'

His glazed eyes went from hers to Raymond's then

back to hers. 'He said for me to st-st-stay,' he stammered.

Judith's heart melted for a moment, for he sounded like a frightened little boy, making excuses to his mother. 'Yes, I know,' she said, sighing and wiping the perspiration from his forehead.

Another attack of shivering struck and Judith decided immediate action was called for. Lying on a marble floor wasn't doing him any good.

'You get under his other shoulder, Raymond, and we'll lift him up on his feet together. Ready? Lift!'

Judith hadn't been a nurse all these years for nothing. She had strong arms and shoulders, along with a good strong spine. Shared, Alex's weight was not too much for them, especially now that he was conscious. They didn't have too much trouble getting him up the stairs and along to the main guest room, though once they lowered him onto the side of the green silk quilt Alex collapsed sideways in a moaning, groaning heap.

'Have you got a pair of pyjamas he can borrow, Raymond?' she asked as she took off his shoes and lifted his feet onto the bed. 'He needs to get these hot, sticky clothes off.'

'I'll go and ask Mrs Cobb. She has some spares for unexpected guests somewhere. But first I'm going to ring Harry. Why don't you undress him and get him into bed while I do that?'

Raymond didn't see her appalled expression because his question was thrown over his shoulder as he strode from the room. It was a sensible enough suggestion, of course, but still she hesitated. Crazy, when she'd undressed hundreds of men.

But not *this* man...

Swallowing, Judith mentally put on her nurse's cap and just got on with it. She did pretty well, too, considering the lack of cooperation she was getting. Still, Alex's delirious state was somewhat of a help. It was impossible to drool over broad shoulders and sheer male perfection when the owner of that perfection was incoherent.

At last she had him stripped down to snugly fitting white briefs, keeping her eyes modestly averted while she rolled him this way and that to finally get him underneath the warmth of the quilt.

'Harry's on his way,' Raymond said as he walked in the room carrying a pair of striped flannelette pyjamas. 'Mrs Cobb says these are brand-new.'

'I don't think he'll be needing them tonight.' Judith frowned at the way Alex was now sweating profusely. 'His temperature keeps going up and down.'

'He looks ghastly. Hope we don't get it.'

'I never get colds or flu.'

'No, you don't, do you?'

'Neither do you,' she pointed out.

'That's because I did when I was younger. I used to get everything. Maybe I've built up an immunity. I think I hear a car. Yes, there's the lights in the driveway. Here, take these pyjamas. I'll go and let Harry in.'

Judith put the pyjamas on top of the chest of drawers which sat against the far wall, then hung up Alex's clothes while she waited, throwing his dirty socks down the laundry chute in the bathroom before putting his shoes neatly in the bottom of the built-in wardrobe.

The main guest room was a lovely, spacious room, decorated in cool greens and warm creams, with lacquered pine furniture which created a cosy cottage look. The only minus to the room, in Judith's opinion, was that the large bay windows overlooked the street and caught the noise of any passing traffic.

Still, the Pascoll home wasn't on any main thoroughfare so the cars were minimal. The bathroom was large too, the tiles pale green with a pattern of dark weeping ferns all over them which made you think of rain forests. Judith had admired them only that day when she'd scrubbed them sparkling clean.

'A new patient for you, Judith?' Harry said as he bustled in, a frowning Raymond in tow. Dr Larson was a short man with a portly stomach and a shock of white hair. He looked a good sixty but was, in fact, only fifty-five. 'Let's have a look at him and see what's wrong.'

Harry was always thorough and left no stone unturned. He took Alex's temperature and pulse, checked his eyes and ears, then listened to his chest, front and back, for ages. Alex surfaced to speak to him a couple of times and take the deep breaths ordered, almost making sense at times.

'A glass of water,' Harry ordered at one stage. Judith brought it from the bathroom and watched as he made his patient down a couple of capsules. Then he gave an injection which looked like antibiotics.

Once administered to, Alex quickly lapsed back into a feverish semi-coma, thrashing around in the big bed, baring a large proportion of his naked chest when he pushed the quilt down a little and flung his arms wide on the pillows.

'Leave him,' Harry said when she went to cover him up again. 'He's hot.'

After he'd finished, Harry took Judith and Raymond out into the hall. 'You've got one pretty sick man there. Looks like the Texas flu. I've had quite a few people with that this past month. It takes a lot of different forms. Often no coughs or runny noses. Patients are just damned sick, with fevers, aches and pains in their joints and muscles, headaches and even hallucinations. I've given him a shot of antibiotics plus something to get his temperature down and calm him at the same time. Give him a couple of paracetamol in six hours, if he's awake.'

Judith nodded and he turned to Raymond.

'Frankly, Raymond, I'd put him in hospital if he didn't have an excellent nurse like Judith here to look after him. Even in the best private hospital, he wouldn't get quality one-on-one care like she can give him. Who is he, by the way?'

'A business acquaintance of mine,' Raymond said. 'Name of Alexander Fairchild.'

'Now if he gets any hotter, Judith,' the doctor advised her, 'you'll have to get his temperature down quick smart with a sponge bath. A shower would be better but I don't want you to risk getting him up tonight while he's the way he is. He might faint or fall over and he's a pretty big fellow. I'll come back in the morning and have a look at him on my way to the surgery. Say around eight-thirty?'

'That would be great, Harry,' Raymond said. 'I won't be here but Judith will, naturally.'

Harry frowned. 'Judith will be alone all tomorrow with him? I don't like the sound of that.'

Neither did Judith. But she knew it wasn't what the doctor meant.

'Mrs Cobb will be here,' she told him. 'And the cleaner comes in tomorrow if I need any help.'

'Oh, that's all right, then. See you in the morning.'

Raymond accompanied Harry downstairs, leaving Judith to her thoughts and her dismay. Harry's tomorrow was hours away for her. The digital clock on the bedside chest said eleven-fifteen. It had already been a long day. An exhausting day. And there would be little sleep for her tonight, if any—something Raymond didn't seem to have given a second thought to.

Yet, for all that, a strange excitement was coursing through her veins and she felt alive in a way she hadn't felt in years. Alex wasn't the only one suffering from a fever.

She walked over to the side of the bed and stared down at him, thinking how vulnerable he looked, lying almost naked in that big bed, unaware in the main of where he was and what he was doing. He muttered something in his delirium which she did not hear properly. She bent and put an ear close to his parted, panting lips.

And then it came again, rasped from a parched-sounding throat. 'Judith...'

Her head snapped up as though he'd struck her. She stared down at him, but his eyes remained closed and she was fairly sure he had no idea she was even in the room.

The trouble was she knew *he* was in the room. Her guilty ghost. Her secret obsession. She tried to block out the memories and the feelings which always came with thinking about him but it was like trying to block out the sun on a hot summer's day.

Automatically, her breathing quickened, drying her mouth and her lips. She licked them in her agitation as she kept looking down at him.

'Judith!' he cried suddenly, the sound dragging at something deep down in her soul.

And then she did something really shocking. She bent back down and licked *his* lips, not hers.

His eyes flung open like a bind shooting upwards, catching her in the act. Stunned and ashamed, Judith held her breath. But there was no scorn in his eyes, no contempt. Only relief, and, yes, something like love.

'Judith.' Almost smiling, he lifted his left hand to hold it briefly against her cheek, but then it fell back down, and so did his eyelids. Panic-stricken, she felt for his pulse, fearing she might not find one, but it was there, slightly irregular but quite strong. He was only asleep.

She doubted if he would remember what she'd done in the morning. But what if he did?

It was a highly agitated Judith who left him for a while to go to Mrs Pascoll's bathroom and collect the things she might need during this long, long night.

CHAPTER EIGHT

AFTER Raymond had gone to bed, Alex settled long enough for Judith to have a shower and change into a warm maroon tracksuit and slippers, much more suitable clothing for sitting and watching a patient through a winter's night. The bedrooms were centrally heated but it didn't seem a good idea to have the thermostat turned up too high in the guest bedroom, since Alex's temperature was a matter of concern.

Besides, it was not in Judith's interests to do anything which would make it necessary for her to give Alex a sponge bath. Just thinking about such a task was perturbing in the extreme.

Once suitably attired, Judith returned with the book she was reading at the moment—a romantic saga set in Ireland—and sank into a comfy armchair in a far corner of the room some distance from the bed. After her previous reprehensible behaviour, she'd decided to remove herself a little from temptation. There was a reading lamp behind the chair, but she also left one of the bedside lamps on, which shone sufficient light on her patient for her to be able to keep a check on his colour and general condition from where she sat.

Luckily, the book was a good one and she was soon distracted from her fears over the present unfortunate situation, finding solace in the world of fiction and fantasy.

The time was approaching two when a sound from the bed sent her eyes snapping up from the page, her heart skipping a beat. But she stayed where she was. Alex was soon threshing about again, moaning and groaning.

Steeling herself, Judith rose and went to his side, her fingers quivering slightly as she held the back of her hand against his forehead. Heavens, he was really burning up this time. She didn't need to take his temperature to know that.

There was no time for thought, or qualms. It was time to act.

Throwing back the bedclothes, she dashed into the bathroom and filled the basin and sponge she had ready with tepid water. Tossing several thick cream towels over her shoulder, she returned and swiftly readied Alex's body for a bed bath, briskly stripping the underpants from his overheated body with not a single thought to her own previously overheated flesh. It seemed she was a nurse first in an emergency, and not a sex-crazed, obsessed fool!

Putting towels under his body was not easy but she managed. 'It's all right, Alex,' she soothed as she started on his face, sponging away the perspiration and stroking back his sweat-soaked hair. His head rocked from side to side as he muttered under his breath. She recognised the odd swear word, which made her smile. She'd heard worse, especially when patients were coming out of anaesthetic.

Judith worked her way down his throat to his shoulders, chest and arms. It was with an oddly clinical detachment that she began to study him as she worked. He had one of those naturally beautiful male bodies which didn't need hours of pumping iron to look good, though no doubt he did do some form of exercise, since his muscles were so well defined and strong. He had a superbly hard, flat stomach and a manly mat of dark curls on his chest which arrowed down past his navel.

Her sponge followed her eyes and suddenly Judith wasn't quite so clinically detached. Alex's tan, she noted with a drying throat, was not all over, his skin paler within the outline of a brief swimming costume. Biting her bottom lip, she started to sponge him down there as well, startled when his flesh immediately responded to what was really a tentative stroke of the damp sponge.

'Oh, no,' she gasped, her stomach contracting at the sight of his rapid arousal. Her hand contracted as well where it was hovering over him, and immediately water from the sponge splashed down on him. Her eyes flew to his, only to find them blinking dazedly open.

But they were not the eyes of a man fully awake, she eventually realised. They were like the eyes of a sleepwalker, a man drugged and dazed. He didn't recognise her. His body was operating on automatic pilot.

Frozen, she didn't know what to do. But she didn't have to decide. He did it for her, one large hand reaching blindly down to clamp over hers, pressing it down, moulding the sponge around him.

His groan of pleasure did dreadful things to her con-

science and for a moment she was tempted to comply
with what he wanted. But it had been one thing to kiss
him—or *lick* him, rather—under cover of his coma-
like state. It was quite another to do this. Such an
action would not only be unethical—she was a nurse,
and tonight he was her patient—but, worse, what if he
remembered something in the cold light of morning?
How could she possibly face him?

His eyes closed again, and gradually his flesh subsided under the coolness of the sponge. Not so his hold
on her hand. It was an iron grip and his fingers had to
be prised open one at a time before Judith could place
his hand back on the bed. Finally, she was able to
resume the sponge bath, and this time she kept well
away from the main danger zone.

But it wasn't Alex's arousal which proved the danger this time. It was her own. No matter how hard she
battled to recapture that clinical detachment, it was
gone. Desire flared as she washed him, the compulsion
to kiss his hot, damp flesh so intense that denial felt
physically painful. She struggled against the devil's
urgings, resisting till her job was done and Alex's skin
was clean and cool to the touch. He had settled back
into a deep sleep and was no longer thrashing about.

She was actually covering up his nakedness with
the sheet when the temptation proved too much for
her. Dropping the sheet around his hips, she bent her
head to press quivering lips to his chest. Her kisses
were gentle, but, for all that, fiercely inflaming. Her
mouth travelled slowly downwards and her head began to whirl. She kissed his ribs, his stomach, his navel. It was only when her lips encountered the edge

of the sheet and Alex groaned that her head jerked upwards.

His eyes were still shut, thank God. But his mouth had fallen open, and his breathing had quickened. Even in his sleep, he had felt her kisses, she realised shakily. And was responding to them. She didn't dare look under that sheet. The very thought twisted her stomach with a mixture of excitement and agitation.

She jumped to her feet and fled to the furthest corner of the room. She curled herself up defensively in the armchair, shoving a fist in her mouth lest she sob aloud with anguish. Would he remember any of this when he woke? she wondered. And if he did would he look at her and see the proof of his last accusation—that she was a deviously wicked woman who engaged in all sorts of kinky sexual activities whilst technically keeping her virginity?

Such a prospect horrified and humiliated her. At the same time she remained hotly aware of the fierce restlessness which still gripped her own flesh. Being physically frustrated to this degree was a new experience for Judith. Guilt over her last foray into mindless passion had kept her sexuality imprisoned for years. She hadn't dated; hadn't sought male companionship in any way; hadn't *wanted* it. Now her skeleton in the closet had well and truly escaped.

She wanted Alex, wanted him with a passion which was almost unbearable.

Her main trouble now was that since she'd decided *not* to marry Raymond she could actually *have* Alex without betrayal, unless one counted betraying her own pride and self-respect. She could even be paid five million dollars for the privilege.

What a corrupting thought!

Judith was tortured by it till just before the dawn, when she slipped into a restless sleep in the armchair, where upon she was further tormented by erotic dreams. Water figured largely in those dreams, as well as starkly sensual sounds coming from wide, gasping mouths.

'Judith.'

She jolted awake with a startled cry, only to find Raymond standing by her shoulder, already dressed for work. 'I'm off to the office. How did the night go? Alex is still asleep, though I think he's stirring.'

Judith scrambled from the chair and tried not to look as instantly flustered and guilty as she was feeling. The sun was creeping in the window nearest to her and the digital clock said twenty to eight.

'He only woke once,' she said quickly. 'I sponged him down a bit and he went straight back to sleep.' Liar, liar, pants on fire! came a taunting rhyme from her childhood. Why don't you tell him the truth? Why don't you tell him you can't marry him?

Alex is right. You're a coward. Always running away from unpalatable truths.

But it's not the right time, she wailed inwardly. I can't hurt Raymond like that. I can't hurt *myself* like that.

It'll never be the right time, countered that other harshly impatient voice which was growing stronger all the time. You'll never tell him, will you? You'll probably end up marrying him just so you don't hurt him and then you'll end up hurting him more. What of your own happiness, you stupid, self-sacrificing, wishy-washy ninny? Aren't you ever going to have what *you* want?

Not if what I want is bad for me, argued a third voice—the voice of common sense.

Pulling herself together, she straightened her crooked clothes and walked with Raymond to the bedroom door, not looking at the bed on the way. 'I think Alex will make a very quick recovery,' she said. 'He's a strong man. A couple of days' rest and he'll be fine to go home.'

'That's good news. Well, I'll see you tonight, Judith, around seven.' He kissed her on the cheek and was off, hurrying down the hall with long, eager strides. Raymond enjoyed going to the office. He enjoyed his work. It was what he lived for.

'Judith...?'

She whirled round at the calling of her name, her heart instantly thudding. Did the hesitation in Alex's voice and the frown on his face mean he didn't recall anything that had happened the night before? She hoped so. Dear God, she prayed so!

'Good morning,' she said with false brightness as she walked over to tuck in the side of the bed. 'You're looking a lot better this morning. A little pale but then what would one expect after a night battling with the Texas flu? The doctor's going to drop in during the next hour. He came to see you late last night, actually, if you remember. His name is Larson. Dr Harry Larson. He's very nice.' Judith knew she was prattling on but she couldn't help it. Her heart was racing and her head whirling.

'Dr Larson?' Alex repeated, frowning and glancing around the room. 'Oh, yes, I remember...sort of...at least...' He was shaking his head as though struggling for memories. 'I remember Raymond telling me to stay, and then...well, nothing much after that, actually. It's a jumble. I do remember you and Raymond helping me up the stairs.'

Judith tried not to look too relieved. 'Yes, that's right. You'd collapsed on the bottom step.'

His eyes on her were suddenly sharp. 'Was it you who undressed me?'

'Raymond helped me,' she lied, and he immediately frowned.

'But it was you who looked after me during the night,' he insisted. 'You stayed here in the room, didn't you? All night. I remember waking once and seeing you in that chair over there, dozing. It was just getting light.'

Judith found the thought that he'd been watching her while she was asleep particularly unnerving. It made her appreciate how vulnerable *he'd* been in his sleep and how unforgivable it had been of her to take advantage of that vulnerability the way she had.

'You were very sick,' she said. 'Someone had to stay with you. Your temperature was sky-high.'

'It was still good of you to look after me like that, Judith,' he said grimly. 'Why did you? If I were you, I would have let me rot.'

'I'm a nurse, Alex,' she said simply, as though that explained it all.

'Mmm.' He didn't seem convinced.

'What do you think you're doing?' she said with alarm when he swung his feet over the side of the bed under the bedclothes and sat up, the quilt slipping dangerously down to expose a good proportion of his naked torso.

'I need to get up and go to the bathroom,' he said. 'And I need a shower. I—' He broke off suddenly, his dark brows knitting together over troubled black eyes. They stared down at that part of his body still thankfully hidden under the quilt, then slowly rose to lock with hers. 'I might be imagining things but did you wash me during the night? I thought it was a dream— I dream a lot about you, Judith—but I seem to vaguely recall something wet and cool stroking over me.'

What to say? Should she admit it? Would that spark further recollections? Maybe she should let him go on thinking it was a dream. No. He might remember the incident more clearly later, and that could be fatal.

'Yes, I did sponge you down once,' she confessed brusquely. 'You were burning up and I had to get your temperature down. Fast.'

'Mmm. Pity I was half-asleep,' he muttered. 'Still, my subconscious tells me it felt good. You wouldn't care to give a repeat performance now that I'm awake, would you?'

Relief that he didn't remember everything quickly turned to tartness. 'You wish!' she snapped. 'Look, I'm off to see to some breakfast for you and to get some fresh sheets for your bed. While I'm gone, take those pyjamas with you into the bathroom and have a quick shower. Don't lock the door and don't overdo it. You'll find you feel as weak as a kitten. After the doctor's gone I'll give you a shave, if you like.'

He rubbed his stubble, which looked far too attractive on him for words. It lent a decided edge to his already harsh handsomeness. He looked broodingly wicked and blatantly sexual sitting there, his tanned nakedness and dark colouring striking a compelling contrast against the cool cream sheets.

'No, wait!' she called out in panic when he went to throw back the quilt.

'Wait for what?' he asked, perplexed.

'Wait till I'm out of the room, damn you!'

Her outburst startled then amused him. 'Am I to take it that the sight of me in my birthday suit is too much for you, Judith?'

'You can take it any way you like,' she returned irritably. Why hadn't she just ignored him and walked out?

'You washed that same naked body last night,' he reminded her.

A guilty heat zoomed into her cheeks, which only increased her irritation. 'That was different,' she said sharply.

'Was it? I wonder... I know I couldn't do the same for you without a great deal of difficulty. Did you wash me all over, Judith? Did I enjoy it?' A light suddenly switched on in his eyes. 'My God, I did, didn't I?'

Judith battled to find a cool voice. 'Men get erections all the time while they're asleep,' she pronounced curtly. 'It means nothing.'

'Then why are you so afraid of seeing me naked this morning? I haven't got an erection now.'

'You have an overdeveloped opinion of your sex appeal, Alex. I was thinking of *your* potential embarrassment, not mine.'

'Then don't, Judith. Nakedness doesn't embarrass me.' He threw back the quilt and stood up, only to find he wobbled so much he had to sit down again. 'Hell, but you're right. I'm like jelly.' His mouth creased back into a sardonic smirk. 'How about a shoulder to lean on while I stagger into the bathroom?'

'Nice try, Alex. I suggest you stay sitting for a minute or two then try again. You'll soon find your feet—a big strapping macho male like you.'

And Judith swept out of the room, frustrated and fuming. Who did he think he was, flaunting himself in front of her like that? The man was not only corrupt, he was the devil incarnate, always tempting her, inevitably tormenting her. So much for his apology last night. It seemed the ruthless seduction routine was back on track, now that his incredibly ill-timed illness had placed him within easy striking distance.

Talk about the fickle finger of fate!

Judith stormed down the stairs and along to the kitchen where she did her best to hide her uncharacteristic flare of temper from Mrs Cobb, who was thankfully already *au fait* with the situation upstairs. Raymond had filled her in over breakfast.

She was all clucking sympathy for Alex, her mother hen nature coming to the fore as she immediately started making up a breakfast tray which would have done Henry the Eighth proud. Alex had already made a good impression on her over dinner last night, it seemed, charming her effortlessly with compliments on her cooking.

Judith was tempted to pull the wool from her eyes but didn't, of course. The woman was clearly enjoying the feeling of being needed by their unexpected guest. It also seemed cruel to point out that Alex wouldn't want to eat half of what she was preparing, so she said nothing and reluctantly went in search of fresh sheets.

By the time she walked into the guest room with her arms full of green linen, Alex was slumped in the armchair she'd slept in, his wet hair showing that he had indeed had a shower, however brief.

He'd half obeyed her, she noted wryly, having put on the long navy and white striped pyjama bottoms, but his top half was still disturbingly bare and even the modest-styled pants were tied perilously low on his narrow hips.

At least he looked thoroughly exhausted. Exhausted male patients, Judith had found during her training years, rarely made a physical nuisance of themselves with members of the opposite sex.

But Alex is not the only problem here, that wretched mischief-making voice reminded her. It's *your* desires we really have to worry about, Judith. Look at the way your eyes are feasting upon him right now—as if he were a piece of death-by-chocolate cake and you the worst kind of chocaholic!

It was to be thanked Alex's intelligent dark eyes were blessedly shut, giving her a moment or two to collect herself. Clearing her throat, she strode efficiently into the room and began stripping the bed. She was instinctively aware of the moment those dark eyes half opened and started watching her. The hair stood up on the back of her neck, making her wish she'd left it down, instead of bundling it up in a prim knot.

'I see the shower knocked some of the stuffing out of you,' she remarked once the bed was properly made and he was still silent. 'That's good.'

Judith pummelled and plumped up the pillows in their fresh pillow-cases with a degree of physical satisfaction. It was like having a punching bag to take her frustration out on.

'I have no intention of putting up with any more nonsense from you, Alex,' she warned him. 'That includes insults. Raymond was fool enough to offer my services to you out of the goodness of his heart. But he meant my nursing services. Nothing else.

'If you have any decency in you at all, you will not resume making disgusting proposals to me and accept that I do not return this rather sick sexual fixation you seem to have developed where I'm concerned. I told you once and I'll tell you again. I am not what you think. I wasn't marrying Simon for his money, and I'm not marrying Raymond for his money.'

Since she was no longer going to marry Raymond at all, that was certainly a correct statement!

'I'm beginning to think you actually believe all that rubbish, Judith,' he said with a weary sigh. 'You're deluding yourself but I'm too tired right now to prove my point. Give me time, though. Now that fate has thrown us together again, I have no intention of giving up on you, and no intention of letting you go through with this travesty of a marriage. I like Raymond too much for that,' he added, with a dark chuckle.

Judith's own laugh carried disbelief. 'You *like* Raymond, yet you're trying to seduce his fiancée?' No way could she break her engagement to Raymond now, she thought, not till Alex was well and truly gone. If she did, he would pounce, and nothing would save her. Nothing!

'I think the boot's on the other foot, don't you, Judith?' he drawled insultingly. 'You're the expert on seduction around here. That shower cleared my head somewhat and last night is not such a fog any more. You have an incredible touch, my sweet. And incredible lips as well, perhaps?' he added, his expression questioning.

Judith's shame was severe, as evidenced by the blush rushing up her neck and into her cheeks.

'You're disgusting,' she snapped. With a bit of luck, she thought desperately, he might think she was just embarrassed, not mortified.

'So that's the way you're going to play it,' he drawled. 'Like the prissy, uptight virgin in a Doris Day movie. How predictable of you, Judith. But how lacking in foresight. You're backing the wrong man, darling. Raymond's a good fifteen years older than I am and not nearly as virile. Having saved up the sex for so many years, I'd imagine you're going to go right off your head when you finally allow yourself to experience the real thing. At least with me you won't be tempted to look to the likes of Mario to keep you satisfied.'

Judith had stiffened at his words. She wished her

overriding response to them were one of disgust and distaste. But that wasn't the case. All she could think of was Alex making love to her over and over, Alex naked in bed with her and she, in turn, allowed to do whatever she liked with him.

Oh, God...

'Has anyone ever told you you're not a very nice man?' she said with reproach quivering in her voice.

'Not since I became a multi-millionaire.'

Judith stared at him. So that was what was behind his predilection for always jumping to the worst possible conclusions about her. He'd become bitterly cynical over the years, especially about women. What he was heaping upon her was perhaps not totally personal. She'd simply become Alex's whipping boy. He was punishing her for the sins of the whole female race.

But understanding his behaviour was not to condone it.

'I pity you, Alex,' she said. 'You've lost all your standards. You think money and sex are all women want, but you're wrong. There are a lot of women who value kindness and tenderness more, not to mention good old-fashioned love. Without love, all the money and sex in the world would soon become less than palatable.

'You like straight talk? Well, I'll give you some. I thought I loved you once. I certainly wanted you like mad. OK, some of that wanting has unfortunately stayed with me. It seems I can't do anything about that. You still spark a sexual response in me. But I don't love you and I won't go away with you, no matter how much money you offer me. Do I make myself clear?'

'Absolutely. You talk about standards but the reality doesn't back you up. Do you think it's nobler to sell yourself in legal prostitution to Raymond than to go to bed with a man you actually *want* to go to bed with? You talk of kindness and tenderness and while Raymond can be considerate and generous towards a business contact like myself he hasn't demonstrated all that much kindness and tenderness towards *you* in my presence. Frankly, Simon did a better job of projecting those qualities, even if it was just a clever façade.'

'You leave Simon out of this!' Judith burst out, torn apart by his accusations and observations.

'Why should I? He's the nail in your coffin, Judith. You spout all that stuff about love and decency but you didn't love Simon any more than you now love Raymond. If you had, you wouldn't have been going to the altar seven years ago a virgin. While I appreciate how titillating Simon would have found that prospect, I know he wouldn't have been doing without sex. Yet you knew that too, didn't you? You simply kept turning a blind eye to his having women on the side.'

He glared at her across the room, scathing in his reproach. 'I appreciate that what you felt for me might have taken you by surprise. I certainly wasn't in your plans. And if I'm strictly honest I can't accuse you of playing the seductress that week. You avoided me like the plague. Neither do I think you had any intention of letting things go as far as they did out in the garden. Our mutual passion simply got out of hand.

'But I still can't come to terms with the fact that you knew Simon was off having it away with his neighbour's forty-year-old wife even while we were just talking together. I find that totally indecent and utterly obscene.'

Judith wasn't sure afterwards how she must have looked at him. All the blood drained from her face. She felt cold and sick and faint all at the same time.

'No!' she rasped, her voice raw as she shook her head from side to side. 'You...you're lying. He wasn't. He wouldn't. He...he didn't. He couldn't. No...' She began to back out of the room, and bumped straight into Mrs Cobb coming in with the breakfast tray.

CHAPTER NINE

'WATCH it!' the housekeeper exclaimed.

Judith only just managed to stop the orange juice from tipping over. 'Sorry,' she muttered. 'I...I wasn't looking where I was going.'

'I can see that. And how's our patient this morning?' Mrs Cobb threw over at Alex, who'd remained seated and silent throughout the small incident. 'Looking a mite peaky, I see. And what are you doing sitting over in that chair? Aren't you cold without a dressing-gown on?'

'Cold?' he repeated, almost blankly, as though his mind was elsewhere.

Judith's mind was a shambles. She could not get over what Alex had said, yet there was no reason for him to lie. The thought that Simon's betrayal of her had been even worse than her betrayal of him made a mockery of her guilt over all these years. At least she could blame her own behaviour on an unintentional and totally confusing infatuation. But to have been doing what Alex had said Simon was doing that night with a much older and *married* woman...!

Alex had implied it wouldn't have been the first time, either. Daggers of dismay stabbed deep into Judith's heart as she recalled the nights Simon had said he couldn't see her because he was working late at the bank.

And then there'd been that incident way back when Simon was still in hospital, the very same day they'd become engaged. She'd come back rather unexpectedly to see him late that evening and that infamous Nurse Pitt, whose reputation for promiscuity was legendary, had been in his room, bending over the bed. She'd quickly pretended to be fixing the bedclothes, but her face had been flushed. She'd hurried out with a guilty look on her face and Simon had immediately confessed that the nurse had made an embarrassing pass at him. Judith now knew exactly what had really happened, and what they'd been doing.

'Judith!' Mrs Cobb said sharply. 'Stop daydreaming and come over here and help me get Alex into bed. He can hardly stand up by himself, let alone walk.'

Judith forcibly snapped herself out of her distress long enough to do just that, but she could not look at Alex, and as soon as possible she made an excuse to leave the room.

But fate was not going to let her escape that easily, for who should be hurrying along the hallway at that moment but Dr Larson?

'No one was downstairs and the back door was open so I just came on up,' he explained. 'How's the patient doing this morning?'

'Much better, Doctor,' she replied with crisp efficiency. Habits did die hard and doctors always made Judith think and act like a nurse first and a feeling female later. 'His temperature did go up during the night but I attended to that with a bed bath, like you said. He rested much more comfortably afterwards and had several hours' sleep.'

'That's good to hear.' He continued walking towards Alex's room and obviously expected Judith to follow. She fell into step beside him, even though her heart had started thudding painfully in her chest. She didn't want to see Alex just now. She needed time to gather herself, and her thoughts.

In the end, a very real panic had Judith grinding to a halt just short of the dreaded door.

'Would you mind if I left you to it?' she said abruptly to the doctor. 'I was just going to lie down for a while when you arrived. I'm really very tired. Mrs Cobb is in there feeding Alex breakfast so you can pass on any instructions for me to her. Oh, and tell her where I am, will you? Now I really must go. I'm dead on my feet.'

She didn't wait for Harry to say another word, just spun on her heels and practically fled down to her room.

She was lying on the bed half an hour later when there was a soft tap on the door.

'Come in,' she said weakly.

Mrs Cobb popped her head in the door. 'Are you all right, Judith? The doctor thought you might be sickening for something, and Alex is worried you might have caught his flu.'

'I'm just tired.' For pity's sake, she thought, didn't it ever occur to any of them that she'd had no sleep to speak of the night before?

'That's a relief. Don't want you getting sick only two weeks before your wedding.'

Judith smothered a groan.

'Anyway, you'll be pleased to know your patient ate a relatively hearty breakfast and the doctor has pronounced he'll live.'

'How nice,' Judith said flatly.

Her lacklustre response brought a frown from the housekeeper. 'You really are tired, aren't you, love? In that case when Betty arrives I'll send her down to the chemist to collect the script the doctor left and I'll attend to the pill-taking and whatever else Alex needs. You just rest.'

'Betty?' Judith repeated, her brain a little fuzzy. 'Oh, yes...' She climbed off the bed and picked up her purse from the dressing table, taking out a fifty-dollar note. 'I want you to give Betty this on top of her Friday money and tell her to take the rest of the day off. Tell her to get her hair done or go to a movie or something. There's nothing for her to do today anyway. I did it all yesterday. Tell her it's a bonus from Raymond.'

'No, I won't. I'll tell her it's a present from you. Raymond wouldn't think to do something like that. You're a sweet girl, Judith.' She took the note, folded it and put it in her apron pocket. 'And very thoughtful.'

And a fool, Judith thought after Mrs Cobb had left. A naïve fool. I believed in Simon's love, believed in *Simon*.

Maybe Alex is right to be cynical about life, and people, she agonised as she lay back down. Maybe we're all basically rotten, me included. Alex clearly believes the human race is vile. How else could he believe such a horrible thing of me?

A sob escaped Judith's throat and she reached out to clutch Peter Panda tight against her. The tears began to flow then, tears of confusion and despair. She cried herself to sleep, the tears remaining on her cheeks long after oblivion had claimed her conscious mind.

But her subconscious raged on. She tossed and turned, sometimes moaning softly, sometimes mumbling confused words and names. Once during the long morning her door opened and a figure stood there, watching her tormented sleep.

Alex's narrowed black gaze glanced around her room, taking in all the soft toys with their soft eyes looking back at him. His lips compressed before his eyes returned to the distraught woman lying on the bed, clutching the toy panda in her arms.

'Damn and blast,' he muttered. His shoulders sagged for a moment, but then they straightened. His eyes hardened again and he turned to make his way slowly back along the hall.

Judith woke with a start to find her door open. She frowned. Surely she had closed it? Had Mrs Cobb opened it? Or Betty maybe? She had an awful feeling that it hadn't been either of them. That it had been Alex.

Why had he come? To talk to her, perhaps? To find out if she really hadn't known about Simon's perfidy?

Her heart leapt with hope till she dismissed such a possibility as futile anyway. For, even if he had come to talk, how would that change anything? He didn't love her any more. He wasn't the same man he'd been seven years ago. He'd become hard and cynical and ruthless. Without conscience, he'd claimed arrogantly. Without true caring.

'You will be mine...' he'd said. But there had been no love in that vow. Only lust. He would hurt her if she gave in to him. Hurt her terribly. She had to keep him at bay, as one would a wild animal. Her own disgustingly weak feelings had to be ignored. Alex was dangerous and destructive.

But oh, so insidiously exciting.

Judith desperately wanted to believe she could resist him. But she didn't have any more faith in herself than she had any longer in the male race. Only Raymond represented goodness and decency to her. Yet it wasn't Raymond she wanted. It was Alex. Alex the beautiful. Alex the bad.

'Oh, Peter,' she cried, clutching her toy friend all the tighter. 'Help me. Tell me what to do!'

Peter's silence was an ominous warning. But there wasn't anything anyone else could do, Judith accepted bitterly. The strength would have to come from within herself. She had to find more courage from somewhere. More pride and more will-power. That was all that would keep her safe.

It was no wonder she was afraid. For experience had taught her she wasn't strong on those three things around Alex.

'I know.' Judith sighed as she swung her feet over the side of the bed and stood up. 'But I'll try to be good. Really I will.' She walked over and shut the door, then locked it. 'And I'll keep right away from him. Mrs Cobb can look after him from now on. I've had it!'

CHAPTER TEN

'I'VE told Alex to stay on over the weekend,' was the first thing Raymond said when Judith joined him in the drawing room for a pre-dinner drink early that evening.

Her fingers tightened around the sherry glass he'd just handed to her. 'Do you think that was necessary?'

'Mrs Cobb says he's still very weak. Too weak to sit up at a table and have dinner tonight. You can't send a man back to a hotel room like that. And he's still far too sick to fly home.'

'And what did Alex say?' True to her resolve, she hadn't been in to see him all day; she'd stayed in her room and pretended she was asleep. Only after Raymond had arrived home had she ventured out of her room, and only to come straight downstairs.

'He said, "Thank you very much, Raymond. I'd like that."'

'I think he's overstaying his welcome,' Judith muttered.

Raymond chuckled. 'You still don't like him, do you? But Mrs Cobb does. She's been fussing over him like mad. She even had Betty wheel a portable television in for him to watch. By the look of the trayful of mugs, glasses and other assorted crockery sitting on top of the chest of drawers, she's been running up and down the stairs all day, bringing him whatever he fancied.'

Judith made a snorting sound. If Alex had any decency, he would have taken a taxi right out of here today. There could only be one reason for his staying on in this house so doggedly. He still hadn't given up his vengeful vow to get her into bed, to *make her his*, as he had so arrogantly put it. Well, she had no intention of being his, or any other man's, not even Raymond's. As soon as she could leave the Pascoll house without distressing him too much, she was out of here!

'Alex is taking advantage of your hospitality, Raymond,' she snapped. 'Not to mention Mrs Cobb's maternal instinct.'

Raymond's wry laugh had her frowning at him. 'What's so funny?'

'I was thinking of what Margaret said to me on the telephone last night when she heard Alex was over for dinner, then today again, when she found out he'd fallen ill and was staying in the house.'

'What did she say?'

'That you and Alex were having an affair and that his illness was just put on so that he could be alone with you. She suggested I spy on you both and find out the awful truth for myself.'

Judith's dismay was acute. This was the kind of thing that made it even more impossible for her to break her engagement to Raymond just yet. Margaret would have a field day, and before she was finished Raymond would be believing her vile lies. Judith knew her conscience could not bear hurting Raymond like that. He was not like Simon. He was a good man. A decent man.

'I've had just about enough of your sister, Raymond,' she said tautly. 'If that isn't the most—'

'Stupid damned thing you've ever heard!' Raymond finished for her. 'Yes, I know. Believe me, I told her straight you didn't even like the man, but she wouldn't listen. She's got some bee in her bonnet and I'm afraid there's no changing Margaret's mind once she gets a bee in her bonnet.'

'She's always going to try to spoil things between us, Raymond,' Judith said, suddenly realising she could use this after Alex left as one of the reasons why she'd decided not to marry him. 'She says things to me when you're not listening, you know. She's always trying to make trouble.'

Raymond sighed. 'I'll speak to her.'

'Do you think that will do any good?' Judith asked unhappily.

'Probably not.'

The telephone rang and they exchanged wary glances. Judith shook her head from side to side. 'I'll bet that's her again.'

Raymond's face tightened, his thin mouth thinning even further. 'If it is, she'll wish she hadn't rung, believe me.'

Raymond stalked off and Judith sank into her chair in front of the fire, feeling infinitely depressed.

Depression was a funny thing. It was such a wearying emotion. All one wanted was to go to bed and pull the bedclothes up over one's head. The present became intolerable and the future just looked hopeless.

Judith didn't feel she had the strength to do more than sip her drink.

Raymond came back with a very troubled look on his face. 'Not Margaret?' Judith ventured.

'No…not Margaret…'

'Who was it, then?' Judith was puzzled. It wasn't like Raymond to be so vague. And he looked genuinely troubled. 'Raymond?' Judith prompted. 'What was it? Is there anything wrong? Can I help?'

'What? Oh, no, Judith, nothing you can do. It was just someone from work. There's a problem down at the factory. I'm going to have to go down there first thing in the morning and sort it out.'

'Oh, Raymond.' Judith groaned her disappointment and growing dismay. Mrs Cobb had Saturdays off and always went out, not returning home till late in the afternoon. The last thing she wanted was to be in the house alone with Alex all day. 'Try to get home as soon as you can, will you?'

'I'm not sure how long I'll be…'

'What kind of a problem is it?'

'A serious one,' he muttered.

'Yes, but *what*, exactly?'

He gave her the oddest look. If she hadn't known better, she might have thought Raymond felt guilty about something.

'I don't think I can explain it,' he said slowly. 'It's rather complicated. I can only hope I'll be able to work it out. If not…'

'If not what?'

His smile was rather wan as he leaned down and

placed a tender hand against her cheek. 'You're a sweet girl, Judith, and I care about you a lot.'

'And I care about *you* a lot, Raymond,' she returned, surprised when tears pricked at her eyes.

His hand dropped away and he looked distracted again. 'Life is difficult, isn't it?' he muttered. 'You simply can't have everything.'

'I'm not sure what you're talking about, Raymond. Are you having money problems?'

'Good Lord, no! What ever made you think that?'

'You mentioned a problem down at the factory...'

'No, it's not money.' He downed a mouthful of whisky and suddenly looked stronger. More like his usual self. 'It's an unfortunate situation with one of the staff. A foreman in the factory. He's been caught stealing stock.'

Judith was surprised. She'd thought it was something much worse. 'Are you going to call in the police?'

'No, I'll settle it myself. He's been with me for a long time and he's always been a good worker. I'll be sorry to lose him.'

Judith could see that Raymond genuinely *was* sorry. More than sorry, actually. He was quite upset, a dark air of distraction possessing him all through dinner. Conversation was desultory at best. After dessert, he excused himself to go up and have coffee with Alex.

'Why don't you come along too?' he suggested at the last moment.

Judith hesitated, then agreed with a shrug. It would look suspicious if she never went near the man, and it was infinitely safer to be in this presence with Raymond as unwitting chaperon.

Ten minutes later she was settled in one of the two armchairs in the guest room, sipping coffee, while Raymond was perched on the end of Alex's bed, dispensing advice to his admittedly still pale and slightly dishevelled-looking guest.

Judith hadn't shaved Alex as promised and the dark stubble which promised an impressive beard had grown considerably. His hair, though too short ever to be seriously messy, was uncombed and sticking up. Now that he was wearing the top half of the striped pyjamas, he looked like an escapee from a chain-gang.

A very sexy escapee, unfortunately.

'I suggest you get yourself up and go downstairs tomorrow,' Raymond was instructing him in that pompous way of his. 'The weather report says it'll be dry and sunny and we have a lovely morning room where the winter sun shines in. You could have a leisurely brunch after which Judith could show you my extensive library. I'm sure you'd be able to find something to read. If not Judith could pop down to the video shop and pick up a couple of movies for you to watch. We enjoy a good movie, don't we, Judith?'

She smiled her assent but said nothing, still irritated by the way Raymond always volunteered her services without consulting her. No doubt he didn't mean any harm by it, but it was annoying. She would not have been able to stand a lifetime of it, that was for sure.

'Do you like movies, Alex?' Raymond asked.

'Don't seem to have much time to watch them, actually.'

'Too busy making money, I suppose.'

'Something like that.'

'How did you get started in real estate?' Raymond went on, and Judith looked up. She was curious about that too but hadn't liked to ask. 'I gather from Judith you started off in finance then went into farming. Your father had some sort of accident, didn't he?'

'That's right. Things were pretty tough for a while because I wasn't much of a farmer. Then one day this property development fellow turned up wanting to buy our whole farm. He'd bought the property on one side of us and had plans for a country-style resort and golf club but needed more ground. After I convinced him to pay the same amount of money for only half our place, he proclaimed me a natural salesman and offered me a job. I wasn't able to take him up on it then but when Karen married the son of the farmer on the other side of us I had my chance to escape without letting anyone down.'

'You've certainly done well for yourself in a short period time,' Raymond said, echoing Judith's thoughts.

Alex shrugged. 'I was lucky, I guess. It turned out this property developer was keen to retire early enough to enjoy the fruits of his endeavours. He said he wanted someone to take over the running of his business and he saw me as his answer. He'd taken a shine to me, I guess.

'Anyway, I went from being his protégé to his right-hand man then to his partner within five years. He's retired now and living in Monaco, with his new twenty-five-year-old wife. I think she's number four.

Greg is not renowned for being a family man. Still, I owe him a lot, I suppose. He taught me everything he knew, even flying.'

Not to mention how to be a first-class bastard, Judith thought as she listened to his story. Fast money. Fast women. Fast everything. No doubt Alex had become addicted to instant gratification and success, and would see any rejection as a challenge to be met, a sale to be made, a mountain which simply had to be conquered.

'Your family must be very proud of you,' Raymond said.

'Proud?' Something in Judith's face suggested his folks weren't too proud of their high-living, high-flying son. 'I think they would have preferred me to settle down to a less demanding job, marry some nice girl and have half a dozen kids.' He looked at Judith then and she could not look away. His dark, penetrating eyes had locked with hers and simply would not let go. 'It might not be too late,' he said determinedly, 'if I can find some nice girl who would have me.'

Judith could not believe his gall! He didn't want to marry her. He didn't want to settle down and have a family. He wanted only one thing from her and it wasn't a vow for better for worse, for richer for poorer, in sickness and in health, till death us do part. The only words he wanted to hear on her lips were 'Yes, Alex', 'Whatever you want, Alex', 'Whenever you want it, Alex'.

If men like Alex or that Greg person ever married, it was strictly for convenience. They traded in their wives on a regular basis. If they had children, it was strictly to provide an heir for their ill-gotten gains. Divorce, not death terminated *their* marriages, of which there were many.

Yet for all that Judith was still bewitched by the way he was looking at her, as though nothing else in the world existed for him but her.

Perhaps that was true, for the moment. He was a passionate man, and she'd more than inflamed his passion by refusing to give him what he wanted. She was the ultimate challenge now, and he meant to win. She could see it in his face, and in his eyes.

Typically, Raymond didn't notice a thing. He even laughed. 'You'll have women lined up around the block, Alex, if and when you decide to audition for a bride. But I won't guarantee the niceness of their character. Wealth attracts the wrong kind sometimes. My sister found herself a right gigolo, I can tell you.'

'Having money can be a problem, Raymond, I'll give you that. But where there's a will there's a way. I will have a nice girl for my wife and no other.' His black eyes narrowed and there was no doubting his ruthless resolve.

So he *did* mean to marry her! The thought took Judith's breath away, and almost made her lose focus on reality.

Raymond clapped him on the shoulder. 'Well, I wish you luck. They're few and far between these days. There's not too many like Judith here. There's not a mercenary bone in her body. My mother left her a nice little sum in her will and what did Judith do? Gave it away to her own mother. And this was before

I asked her to marry me, too. But, as I said, women like Judith are rare.'

'I'm beginning to appreciate that,' Alex said ruefully, his eyes fixed on her face. She tried to look away but could not.

Raymond appeared to drift off into his thoughts for a few moments before snapping out of them. Clearing his throat, he stood up and glanced over at Judith, who dropped her eyes to her cup just in time.

'I might have an early night, Judith,' he said. 'No, don't get up. Stay and talk to Alex for a while. I'm sure he can do with some company. Goodnight, you two. Be good.'

It was the worst thing he could have said before walking out, for Judith never felt like being good when alone with Alex. In the beginning when she'd first met him, the sexual urges he'd inspired in her had brought confusion and guilt and self-disgust. Now they just brought self-disgust. She knew darned well what she wanted and there was no hiding behind ignorance or bewilderment.

Recognising the intensity of her susceptibility, Judith rose and went to leave. Alex immediately leapt out of the bed and barred her escape by closing the door then leaning against it, his hand on the knob.

'Get out of my way,' she choked out, upset by the emotion which automatically raged through her at his aggressive actions. Once, she might have thought it was fear. Now she knew it was excitement.

'You must listen to me, Judith.'

Her laugh had a hysterical edge to it. 'Since when did you ever want to *talk* to me, Alex?'

'Since always,' he said with astonishing fervour. 'Remember the night of the party? Remember how long we talked, how much we enjoyed each other's company even when we were doing nothing but talking?'

'Men like you use talking to lead to what you really want.'

'Which is what?'

'Winning.'

'Oh, Judith, Judith, what have I done to you? God, I can't tell you how sorry I am for believing such vile things about you. My only excuse is that I'd become so jaded over the years regarding feminine virtue. You have no idea what some women will do for money. But I see now you're not that type of girl. You're good and sweet and kind. I could cut out my tongue for the things I said to you.

'Please say you forgive me, Judith. I've been in hell all day, ever since I realised you were ignorant of Simon's true character.'

'Don't try that tack with me, Alex. It won't work.'

'Then what *will* work?' he countered passionately. 'Tell me what to do and I'll do it! Tell me what to say and I'll say it! I still love you, Judith. Surely you must know that?'

'You don't know the meaning of the word love, Alex.'

'I know it's not the lukewarm affection you hold for Raymond. Or the proprietorial yet insensitive way he treats you in return. Does he know what he's getting with you, Judith? Does he suspect that underneath the cool little virginal façade you're really a very passionate woman?

'My God, I've never forgotten how you responded to me that night. At present, I am clinging to the hope that you've stayed untouched since then because you've never met a man who could do for you what I can do. Am I right?'

'How typically arrogant of you, Alex. What are you going to do? Grab me and kiss me senseless? Reduce me to a mindless sexual puppet just to prove your point? How brave of you. How noble. How very endearing.'

Was it that last taunt which got to him? Whatever, his expression changed from fierce determination to one of an almost despairing frustration. 'I *can't* let you marry him.'

Judith paled at the underlying threat in his words. 'If you say anything to Raymond, I will never forgive you. I promise you, Alex. *Never!*'

'You leave me no choice.'

She left *him* no choice? He left *her* no choice!

Judith swallowed and said the words she didn't want to say to him. For she knew it would only open Pandora's box.

'I'm not going to marry Raymond,' she confessed bleakly. 'I simply haven't told him yet.'

The instant and intense joy in Alex's eyes was hard to ignore. 'You're not?'

'I'm not. And it has nothing to do with you. I've simply decided we aren't right for each other. But that malicious sister of his has been saying some potentially damaging things about you and me. She saw us together the other night at her party and jumped to all the wrong conclusions. So I'm going to wait till you're out of this house and out of our lives before I break the engagement. I don't want another betrayed man on my conscience.'

'Simon wasn't betrayed.'

'Oh, yes, he was. Regardless of what he did to me, I betrayed him. We were going to be married and he thought I loved him.'

'You loved *me*,' Alex insisted in a belligerent tone. 'You still love me.'

'No,' she denied firmly. 'I don't. I don't even like you.'

'I could change that, if you'd give me a chance.'

She laughed. 'That would be like diving into a pit full of rattlesnakes with the assurance from a medicine man that I was immune to their bite. You're a predator, Alex. You'd destroy me.'

'I'd *love* you.'

'No, you'd *make* love to me. That's all.'

'Don't belittle the power of making love, Judith. Making love can lead to loving.'

'Pardon me if I'm not convinced of that.'

'Then give me the chance to convince you. That's all I ask. Hell, Judith, it's what you want too. Stop denying it!'

Judith felt heat gather within her body at the thought. 'You...you expect me to *let* you make love to me?' she asked shakily.

'Yes, damn it! Why not? Since you're not going to marry Raymond, there's no betrayal. He'll never know. If you find afterwards you don't want anything more to do with me, then I promise to let you go...without another word.'

She stared at him and saw the trap. Would she be able to walk away from him afterwards, if his love-making was as magical and powerful as she feared it would be? Those drum beats began echoing in her head, throbbing with the promise of pleasures as yet unknown.

'Don't be a coward, Judith,' he whispered, in much the same way as that inner voice had been whispering to her for days. 'Take a chance. What have you got to lose?'

Only my sanity...

She looked away from him and those magnetic black eyes. She swallowed and tried to think straight.

'Think about it,' he suggested, his tone switching abruptly from silk to steel. 'But I'll want your answer first thing in the morning. If it's no, I'll be leaving. I can't torture myself like this any longer.'

Surprise made her eyes blink wide as they jerked back to his. Did he mean it? Was being near her and not having her such torture for him? It was a beguiling and bewitching thought.

'All right,' she agreed tautly, knowing that even with those two words she was admitting an awful lot. 'I...I'll think about it. Now...can I leave?'

For a long moment she thought he *was* going to reach out and grab her and kiss her senseless. But he didn't. In the end, he stepped aside and opened the door.

All the breath left her lungs in a rush as she fled through the doorway and down to her room where all those beady black eyes gave her no more peace than her own hopelessly whirling head. They watched patiently while she paced agitatedly around the room.

'What should I do?' she asked them all at last. 'Tell me, for pity's sake.'

But there were still no answers to soothe her fears. She was on her own.

Judith scooped in a deep breath and tried to think clearly. Maybe Alex really did love her. It was possible that his feelings encompassed more than lust. But it was also possible that they didn't.

And what of her own feelings? What were they? Love, or lust?

She wished she knew.

Two things could come out of making love with Alex, she decided. A greater happiness than she'd ever thought possible or a greater misery than she'd ever known. And she'd known plenty when Simon had been killed.

Time to make a decision. Should she or shouldn't she?

Judith tried to weigh up the balance before suddenly laughing. Silly girl. There really wasn't a choice, was there?

Time to take a chance.

On love.

CHAPTER ELEVEN

THE morning room was indeed a pleasant room to breakfast in, Judith thought as she sat at the round glass-topped table and sipped a second cup of coffee. The huge semicircular north-facing windows caught the morning sun in the winter, which warmed the air and the cork floor, and provided enough light for the myriad indoor plants. Lush ferns hung from baskets overhead and potted palms filled every corner.

It was like a small conservatory and at nine-thirty that morning was warm and cosy. Mrs Cobb was gone for the day. Raymond had left for the factory, apologetic again about his absence on a Saturday. Judith was not to expect him home till later afternoon, as he would have to make sure of his facts before taking action. He didn't want to be sued later, he'd said. He would ring, he'd promised, before lunchtime.

Alex hadn't made an appearance downstairs as yet, thank heavens, and Judith didn't feel inclined to go upstairs to his room. Mrs Cobb had taken a breakfast tray up before she'd left for her day off, and declared the patient to be well and truly on the mend.

Judith didn't doubt it. He was as strong as an ox. Any other man might have been laid low with that virus for a week, but not Alex. He'd thrown it off and recovered within forty-eight hours.

Alex…

The same questions tormented her this morning as they had last night. Was he sincere in his passion? Or did he just want to finish what they'd started seven years ago?

There was no way to be sure. The only thing Judith was sure of was her own physical need for him. Her desire.

'Good morning.'

Her eyes shot up from where they'd been staring blankly into her near-empty cup. Alex was standing in the doorway, dressed in a grey silk dressing gown and, she suspected, not much else. There were no navy striped pyjama bottoms peeping out from underneath the ankle-length robe, nor a collar in the deep V neckline. Just bare tanned flesh and dark, disturbingly damp curls. It was obvious he'd come downstairs fresh from a shower.

Her own shower that morning had been long as she'd mulled over her decision of the night before and worried over what Alex might suggest when she said yes. Would he take her back to his hotel room? He couldn't possibly mean to make love to her *here*.

'Where did you get the grey silk?' she asked thickly by way of a return greeting. 'No, don't bother to answer. I know it already. Mrs Cobb.'

'I paid for it,' he defended himself, smiling wryly as he came into the room. 'Where shall I sit?'

She waved him into a bucket cane chair on the other side of the room which was catching full sunshine. It had a small square table next to it. He sank back into the deep, sun-warmed cushions and sighed his satisfaction. 'Good choice. Now all I need is another cup of coffee and life will almost be perfect. That is, of course, if you're going to give me the answer I want to hear this morning.

'Are you?' he added when she remained silent and staring.

She just kept looking at him. He'd shaved, she noticed. In fact he looked cool and relaxed and so sexy she could hardly think straight. Her decision of the night before seemed shocking in the clear morning sunshine and she found it impossible to simply say yes. Yes, I want to take that chance. Yes, I want you to make love to me. Yes. Yes. Yes.

'I'll get you that coffee,' she said in strangled tones, and abruptly stood up.

Out in the kitchen, she clattered the crockery, spilled the coffee-beans, then had to load sugar and milk on a small tray alongside a cup of black instant because she couldn't remember how Alex had his coffee. Everything rattled as she carried the tray into the room and placed it on the side-table next to him.

Alex's hand closed firmly over her wrist and when she looked up at him he said, 'Leave it. I don't want any stupid damned coffee. I just want you, Judith.'

And then he was pulling her down into his lap, and his arms were going round her and his mouth was covering hers.

For a brief moment, she froze. She had wanted to be strong this morning. And firm. She'd been going to say yes, but that any lovemaking was to be delayed till after they left the Pascoll house.

But it was impossible to be strong and firm with Alex's arms around her and his lips prising hers open. She gasped under the impact of his hotly invading tongue. When she tried to pull back a little, Alex would have none of it. He gathered her even closer and his kiss deepened, and finally her starving soul could no longer be denied. She moaned and melted into him, wrapping her arms around his neck and kissing him back with a fervour just short of desperation.

Alex didn't seem to mind. He groaned his own satisfaction and matched her passion in a series of kisses which left her panting and light-headed.

'Judith,' he whispered into her hair when at last he let her come up for air. 'Oh, Judith...' He cradled her head under his neck and her eyelashes fluttered closed. She sighed her total surrender to him.

It was while he was cuddling her close to his heart and stroking her back that he grew strangely still. The hand that had been stroking up and down her spine oh, so sensuously stopped in mid-stroke. The muscles in his arms stiffened.

She was about to ask him what was wrong when he tipped her chin up and claimed her mouth once more. She whimpered under the urgent surgings of his tongue and soon she didn't want to ask him anything. Her hands, which had slipped down from his neck, slid inside his robe, her palms pressed flat against his chest. His skin was hot and his heartbeat very rapid. It came to Judith then that Alex was not going to be able to stop. *They* were not going to be able to stop.

She was still startled when he suddenly stood up and began carrying her from the room. 'Where…where are we going?' she asked.

But she already knew. Upstairs. To his bedroom. To his bed.

Judith buried her face into his neck and prayed for God's eternal mercy and forgiveness. This was not what she'd intended to happen this morning.

'Don't hurt me,' she cried softly when he lowered her feet to the floor beside his bed. It wasn't made, she noted dazedly. But the guilt was thrown right back as though the bed was waiting for them.

'Never,' he reassured her, and before she could draw another breath he began taking her clothes off, first the top of her tracksuit, then her bra.

Judith was taken aback by his lack of hesitation, plus his ability to focus on one thing and no other. Her body.

'You are so beautiful,' he said as he began easing the tracksuit bottoms down over her hips, bending to kiss the tip of one peaked pink nipple at the same time.

An uncontrollable quiver ran through her.

'Kick off your slippers,' he ordered when the tracksuit bottoms dropped to her ankles. 'And step out of the pants.'

She obeyed him instinctively and was soon standing before him in nothing but an inadequate scrap of pink stretch satin. His gaze momentarily raked over her, hot and hungry, then he scooped her up in his arms and laid her gently down on the cool green sheets. He peeled her panties down her legs with an expression almost of reverence on his face.

Judith watched with widening eyes as he disposed of the grey silk robe, revealing his own aroused nakedness. When he stretched out beside her on the bed she began to shake, anticipation of what was to come dampening her earlier wild desire and bringing a tense apprehension.

'It's all right,' he soothed, stroking her flanks as though she were a flighty horse. 'I won't hurt you. I love you. You're going to be my wife.'

He spent an infinitely long time relaxing her, then arousing her again, taking her slowly beyond fear into a world she had briefly visited once before where the mind ceased to function except in its blind concentration on her senses, and her sexual needs.

An urgency grew within her, a fire burning deep inside. The more Alex touched her, the hotter that fire became. His lips joined the fray, sucking on one of her aching nipples at the same time as his hand explored her intimately. Her hips started arching from the bed in a silent invitation for more invasion than just his fingers. She wanted *him*, filling her, making her whole.

'Alex...please,' she pleaded, her head threshing from side to side on the pillow.

He probed carefully, gently, Judith flinching at first then tensing even further as the feeling of painful pressure increased. He was too large, she thought in panic as he persisted, inch by agonising inch.

'Relax,' he told her, tension in his voice.

She did, and a surprised gasp of pleasure escaped her lips as he suddenly slid right in to the hilt. A tremor ran through him as he relaxed himself.

'That doesn't hurt any more, does it?' he murmured, cupping her face and kissing her softly on the lips.

She felt shy under his loving gaze. 'No,' she said softly.

'Not at all?'

'Not at all,' she repeated. 'It feels...good.'

'You feel more than good, my darling,' he said ruefully. 'Put your arms around me. And your legs. That way you won't end up with too many bruises. I hope.'

Her arms moved around his back, her fingers curling over his shoulders. She lifted her legs to wrap them high around his waist, her body moulding itself perfectly to his as nature had fashioned.

He rocked into her gently at first, then with more vigour, his movement gradually adopting a powerful rhythm. The fire within her grew hotter and hotter. Judith gasped, then groaned. It was too much. Too much. Then suddenly the flames erupted in one last conflagration and her mouth gaped wide. Her back arched, and as everything exploded inside her she cried out.

Alex's arms tightened around her wildly pulsating body. Then he too cried out, every muscle in his body trembling uncontrollably as he climaxed then collapsed on top of her.

The flames died down as quickly as they had been ignited, leaving Judith feeling slightly seared in his sweat-soaked arms. Was it always going to be like that? she wondered in awe. Would she *survive* if it was always going to be so mind-blowing?

Gradually, the scorched sensation subsided, to be replaced by a deep feeling of physical contentment. A slow smile of blissful satisfaction spread across her face, and she was still smiling when Alex levered himself up onto his elbows and looked down into her glowing face.

'You're incredible, do you know that?' he murmured.

'I was thinking the same of you,' she returned, her heart overflowing with emotion. He'd been so right to say that making love could lead to love. It could, especially when the love had been there all along, just waiting for the right expression.

'I do love you, Judith,' he said.

'Yes,' she answered on a sigh.

'You haven't said you love me back,' he reminded her.

She said nothing, merely smiled.

'You want me to suffer a while longer, is that it?'

Judith blinked her shock.

'No, of course not,' he amended quickly, with a remorseful edge to his voice. 'You're not like that, are you? It's only self-centred, selfish bastards like me who think in terms of blind vengeance. I'll try to be more like you in future, my darling. You *are* my darling, aren't you?' he whispered as he bent to kiss her softly on the mouth.

Her lips quivered, and she nodded.

'Say you love me.'

'I love you,' she whispered, and her heart contracted. For, having said the words out loud, she'd really taken the plunge and put her love for him on the line. Her happiness was in his hands now.

'Never stop loving me,' he insisted with a passion

that Judith still found a little frightening. 'I'll make you happy, I swear. We'll have babies together. And grow old together. I'll never stop loving you, Judith. Say you believe me.'

'I do,' she said.

'I'm going to make love to you again now,' he promised fiercely.

And he did. Slowly and sensuously.

Her pleasure was different this time. Not quite so incandescent, but very, very satisfying nonetheless, the fire now thoroughly quenched. Afterwards, they showered together, and amazingly, the touching soon started again. The fire hadn't really gone out, Judith realised in awe of her own and Alex's quickly renewed desire. It had been secretly smouldering, waiting for either one of them to stoke it into life once more.

Alex snapped off the water and suggested they return to bed once more, where he encouraged her to be more adventurous, showed her what gave him pleasure, complimented her when she did whatever he suggested. For her part, Judith found great excitement in kissing him all over, loving the way his flesh reacted to her mouth and tongue. His nipples hardened. His stomach trembled. The lion of his manhood roared.

'Get on top,' Alex ordered with a raw groan.

She could not help it. She hesitated.

'You'll like it,' he said thickly. 'I promise.'

She didn't at first. She felt shy and vulnerable. She simply could not bring herself to move and told him so. He said that was fine by him and reached up to play with her breasts, kneading the swollen mounds then plucking at her tight, hard nipples till in the end she simply could not stay still. Her body had developed a will of its own. Her hips began to rise and fall, the sword of his flesh moving in and out of her silken scabbard. Judith had never felt anything like it.

Alex seemed to be liking it as well, for he started groaning and his hands dropped from her breasts to lie in limp ecstasy on the bed. His hips began to grind in counterpoint to hers. Up to her down. Down to her up. Gloriously bitter-sweet sensations besieged her. It was going to end soon. She could feel it coming. But she didn't want it to end. She wanted it to go on for ever.

Her head tipped back. Her eyes closed. Her lips parted.

And it was while she was in this state of tensely erotic ambivalence that a voice—sharp and shrill— shattered her new, wonderful world to pieces.

'Didn't I tell you?' Margaret shrieked. 'Oh, my God, Mario, look at them! Look at *her*!'

Judith's eyes flung wide open as her head snapped round to take in the two people standing in the doorway, Margaret sneering and Mario leering over his wife's shoulder. Mario's oily eyes narrowed on her naked form and he purred, 'I am, Marge. I am.'

Alex swore and quickly rolled away from the smirking onlookers, tipping a white-faced Judith into relative privacy by shielding her with his body. She wanted to cry out at his abrupt withdrawal, then to cry. Oh, dear God!

'Get out!' Alex roared over his shoulder. 'You've seen what you came to see, you jealous bitch. Now get the hell out of here!'

'You mean I've seen what you *wanted* me to see,' she countered nastily. 'You wanted me to do your dirty work for you, didn't you? I suggest you listen to this, Judith, so you'll know the sort of man you're dealing with. Your darling lover boy doesn't want to be your little bit on the side. He doesn't want you marrying Raymond, which is fine by me, but I imagine it rather spoils *your* plans, you two-timing trollop.

'I was here earlier when you were canoodling with this creep down in the morning room. But you didn't see me. Lover boy did, though. He saw me all right and knew I'd be back. He even smiled at me, the conscienceless bastard. Can you imagine that? There he was, kissing my brother's fiancée, and he smiles at *me* before kissing you again!'

Judith surfaced from the drowning horror of her humiliation to be hit in the face with a further tidal wave of horror.

'And what did lover boy do after I left?' Margaret continued scathingly. 'Made sure you were thoroughly compromised, with no doubts at all as to the vile carnality of your relationship. Of course, he expected me to return with Raymond. Which I would have...if I could have found him,' she finished irritably.

'So she brought me as a witness instead,' Mario piped up with a smarmy smile which clearly indicated that he was relishing the moment, and the melodrama, not to mention the show.

Judith wanted to die. She clutched the sheet over herself and stared at Alex with distress and disbelief in her face. He didn't look remorseful, simply furious, his glittering black eyes glaring a dark frustration at Margaret and Mario.

'Alex, you didn't,' she choked out. 'You couldn't have. Tell me you couldn't have…'

Alex swore again. But not before she'd seen a flash of guilt cross his face.

'You did,' she said weakly.

'I think we'll go now, Mario,' Margaret said smugly. 'I think we've seen all there is to see here, and said all there is to say. Needless to add, we'll be speaking to Raymond as soon as we can locate him. If you're wise, I'd suggest that *you* two get the hell out of here. You, dear Judith, and your wonderfully sensitive and trustworthy lover. If you still want him, that is,' she added with a cackling laugh.

Alex groaned as they swept out of sight and down the stairs. 'Stop jumping to the wrong conclusions, Judith,' he begged, taking her by her shaking shoulders before she could flee the bed. 'I did it for *you*. I saw her standing there, watching us, and I knew she'd run off and tell Raymond straight away that we were already lovers. I was afraid you'd fall apart from having hurt Raymond and never let me prove to you how much I loved you.'

'And you thought taking me to bed in this house, knowing that any moment the man I was going to marry could walk in, would show me how much you *loved* me?' she asked, her tone incredulous.

'Look, I thought I had nearly two hours before Raymond could possibly arrive. The factory is an hour's drive away. I didn't think of Margaret going home and trying to ring him. I certainly didn't think she'd come straight back here without him. Hell, I was going to stop before Raymond could see us together like this.'

'And you think that makes it all right? That the end justifies the means?'

'In this case…yes.'

'Oh, Alex…Alex…'

'Goddamn it, Judith, I love you. I couldn't risk you escaping from me again.'

She was shaking her head at him. 'You mean you couldn't risk not finishing what you started seven years ago. Love had nothing to do with it. What happened here in this bed was pure lust on your side. If you loved me, you would have stopped and explained about Margaret, then faced Raymond with the truth. You would not have shamed me like this.'

'It wasn't like that! I told you, I didn't expect her to show up again this quickly. I certainly didn't want her to catch us in the act. Give me credit for some sense of decency.'

'Decency!' She could not believe he would dare use the word after what he'd done, after the way he'd allowed that vile man and woman to see her. What should have been a beautiful private moment had been turned into an ugly and very public circus. She felt sick just thinking about it. She felt sicker thinking about how Raymond would look at her once he found out what had happened. No doubt Margaret would paint a truly appalling picture, with Mario adding his own disgusting two bobs' worth. She could still feel his eyes sliding over her, those leering, oily eyes.

Nausea rose in her throat. 'Oh, God, I have to get out of here,' she choked. 'I can't stay here.'

'Running away again, Judith?' Alex threw at her as she scrambled from the bed, dragging the sheet with her.

She turned on him, spitting fire. 'Don't you dare talk to me about running away. I wish to God I'd run away the first time I ever clapped eyes on you. I am *not* running away. I'm merely removing myself from this house. I doubt Raymond will want me in it any more, don't you? My God, when I think of what he's going to feel when Margaret tells him.'

Tears flooded her eyes and Alex groaned. 'You didn't mean to hurt him, damn it!'

'But I did. And so did you.'

'He's a grown man. He'll survive.'

'No thanks to us!'

'I love you, Judith. Don't go. Stay and we'll face Raymond together.'

Her shudder showed the horror that the mere thought of such a confrontation evoked in her. 'I can't. I have to get out of here.'

'Where are you going?'

'Anywhere.'

'Where exactly is anywhere?' he persisted, and Judith could see he wasn't going to give up.

'To a friend's place,' she said.

'What friend? Where can I find you? You might as well tell me, Judith,' he said stubbornly. 'Once you get over the shock of this, you'll see I didn't mean to humiliate you, or hurt Raymond.

'I'm rich now,' he added when he saw her hesitate.

'It's not like the last time. I'll find you, no matter where you go.'

Her shoulders sagged in defeat. She began shaking her head. She didn't have any friends. She hadn't made any in seven years. She'd hidden herself away here with her hurt and her shame. Now they were to be her constant companions once again.

'To Joyce,' she lied in desperation. 'I'm going to Joyce.'

'Who's Joyce?'

'Raymond's secretary.'

Alex frowned. 'The woman with Margaret at the party?'

'Yes, that's right.'

'You didn't seem all that friendly with her from what I remember.'

'Well, you're wrong. She's a nice person. And a good friend.

'Fair enough. I'll stay here and explain things to Raymond when he gets home. And then I'm going to ring you at this Joyce's place, OK?'

'Whatever you like,' Judith said dully.

He made a move towards her but she stopped him with a glance.

'I'm truly sorry, Judith,' he said, and oddly enough sounded it.

'So am I,' came her reply, wrenchingly torn from her. 'So am I.'

CHAPTER TWELVE

JUDITH could feel Alex's eyes upon her as she climbed into the taxi. He was watching her from where he was standing at the front door. He hadn't tried again to persuade her to stay, perhaps recognising her total horror at the thought of facing Raymond. But whenever their eyes had met she'd been disconcerted by the look of disappointment on his.

'Mascot airport,' she told the taxi driver, then sank back into the seat, her eyes closing.

'Which terminal, love?'

'International.'

'Business or holiday?'

'What? Oh, holiday...'

Some holiday, she thought as the taxi driver fell blessedly silent and sped off. But it was the only place she could think of to go. She would take the first flight to London she could get. There should be plenty on a weekend. Thank God she had her passport ready.

You *are* running away again, a small voice whispered deep inside her. You're a coward, just like Alex said you were.

Judith cringed at the thought. No one liked being called a coward, least of all when it was probably true.

Where had this lack of courage come from, she wondered painfully, this fear of confrontation?

From her father, she realised with painful acceptance. He'd been a nice man but a weak one. Her mother had hen-pecked him to death around the house, and he'd simply buckled under rather than fight back. He'd taken the line of least resistance, till his wife had lost all respect for him and he'd lost all respect for himself. Judith knew she took after him in nature as well as looks. But the last thing she wanted was to become the cowed, crushed, colourless individual her father had been at the time of his death.

She'd made a mistake in going to bed with Alex in Raymond's house. But she'd made a bigger mistake in not breaking her engagement as soon as she'd known marriage to Raymond was impossible. In a way, she'd made her own bed by not facing the truth and not acting honestly and honourably. Raymond did not deserve to hear about what she'd done from anyone other than herself. The least she could do was mitigate Margaret's viciousness by explaining what had really happened, and why she'd done what she'd done.

As for Alex... No matter what *he'd* done, she did love him. So she had to go back and face him as well, and find out once and for all exactly how deep his feelings for her were. How could she possibly not do that? She must be insane, running away like this.

'Go back!'

The taxi driver's head swivelled round. 'Pardon?'

'I said, go back. I want to go back.'

His expression showed his exasperation. 'Are you sure, lady?'

'Yes. Yes, I'm sure.'

Sighing, he negotiated an abrupt U-turn which made Judith's stomach jump into her mouth. Or was it fear of what was to come that propelled her heart into a feverish race? The thought of how Raymond would look at her, now that Margaret would have done her worst?

Still, she had to do it. It was the only decision she could live with.

Her agitation increased as Raymond's street drew near. By now he would know the awful truth. Margaret's version of it, that was. He might even be at home.

The taxi swung into the leafy avenue and Judith's worst fears came to fruition. Alex was standing on the footpath outside the house and Raymond's Mercedes was at the kerb. Raymond was just getting out from behind the wheel, and Joyce was emerging from the passenger side. What on earth was *she* doing here? Judith wondered.

She groaned her dismay. Raymond must have taken Joyce down to the factory this morning. Maybe Alex had contacted him there and asked him to come home. It looked as if he'd only just arrived. With a bit of luck Margaret might not have caught up with him yet and Judith could be the first to tell him what had happened.

No, that couldn't be right. She'd only been gone twenty-five minutes, not enough time for Raymond to drive back from the factory. Now she wasn't at all sure what was going on. Still, whatever the reason for Joyce's presence, the last thing Judith wanted was another person to witness her humiliating confession.

Though maybe it was too late for a confession. The awful suspicion that Raymond already knew everything was growing. The only thing that could make this situation worse would be for Margaret and Mario to show up.

This last thought had hardly formed when a black car came speeding around the corner at the other end of the street, swerving into the kerb and screeching to a ragged halt behind Raymond's car. Judith recognised the black sedan as the Jaguar Margaret had presented to her gigolo groom on their wedding day.

She could hardly believe her bad luck. God was really making her suffer this time. The temptation to tell the taxi driver to drive on was fierce, but she resisted. Running away was not on her agenda any more.

She directed the driver to park in front of Raymond's car, paid him, and climbed out just in time to face the five of them, grouped on the pavement and all staring at her with various expressions. Raymond was frowning, Joyce looked tense and tight-mouthed, while Margaret could barely hide her malicious glee as she clung to a smirking Mario's arm.

It was Margaret's overt hatred which swept the sick butterflies from Judith's stomach. She straightened her spine, squared her shoulders and looked right back at them all with dignity and without obvious fear.

'Thank you,' she said to the driver politely when he placed her red suitcase beside her on the pavement before moving off.

It was only then that she glanced straight at Alex, who was standing to one side. Their eyes met, and she realised, in a blinding flash of recognition, how much he cared about her. For there was nothing in his face but a joyous relief that she had returned, and an overwhelming pride in her decision. His eyes gleamed with admiration. When a softly approving smile pulled at his mouth, she found herself smiling back at him.

'My God, just look at them,' Margaret sneered. 'Didn't I tell you, Raymond? They have no shame. Now you can see it for yourself—smirking at each other as though they've done something special instead of rutting away like animals behind your back and making an utter fool of you.'

'If you don't shut your filthy mouth, Margaret,' Raymond snapped, 'I'll shut it for you. I seriously regret even ringing you now. Didn't you hear a word I said over the phone? I told you to keep out of it. Why race over here, damn it, if not to make trouble? Believe me when I tell you I can handle my own affairs. I certainly don't need an interfering trouble-maker like you poking your nose in where it's not wanted. God help you if you do it with Joyce like you did it with Judith.'

Do it with Joyce?

Judith was still trying to work out exactly what was going on when Raymond amazed her further by walking towards her with his hands outstretched. A tiny seed of hope blossomed within her thudding chest. He didn't look at all angry with her. If anything, he looked...sympathetic.

'Judith,' he murmured gently, and took both her

hands in his. 'I'm so glad you came back. Poor Alex was beside himself.'

Poor Alex? Wasn't he angry with Alex either? Judith frowned at this astonishing turn of events. She wasn't a stupid girl and one and one was certainly not making two here. Raymond was not the sort of man to take rejection, or deception, lightly.

She glanced over Raymond's shoulder at Alex, who was looking mighty pleased with himself.

Judith's bewilderment grew. What on earth had he said to Raymond to make him understand? What lies had he told to justify his own less than lily-white behaviour, not to mention hers?

'I am not trying to make trouble this time, Raymond,' Margaret insisted. 'What I told you was true. Why don't you believe me, you stupid man?'

'Hold your tongue, woman!' he ground out, whirling round to glare at his sister. 'For one thing, we're in public. For another, you don't really know what's going on here.'

Margaret's pale eyes narrowed venomously on Judith. 'But I saw them with my own eyes!' she hissed at her brother. 'They were naked in bed together, and they were doing it.'

'If you spent a little more of *your* time naked in bed and doing it, Margaret,' her brother returned savagely, 'then we wouldn't have to be subjected to your jealous and malicious interfering.'

Margaret's mouth dropped open, as did just about everyone else's. Judith was stunned by Raymond's defence of her, not to mention his attack on his sister. Even Alex looked surprised.

'If you must cast stones at anyone here,' Raymond swept on, 'then cast them at me. I betrayed Judith first. Joyce, come over here,' he ordered peremptorily, and held out his hands to his decidedly nervous-looking secretary. Hesitantly, she came forward to take her employer's hands.

Judith was finding it hard to grasp Raymond's words. *He* had betrayed her first? What was he talking about?

Her confusion only lasted till she witnessed the warm smile Raymond bestowed on Joyce and the almost besotted look his secretary gave him in return. The penny dropped with a thud. Joyce was madly in love with her boss. *She* was the woman he'd had an arrangement with all these years, and it hadn't stopped with his engagement to another woman!

Despite the delicious irony of the situation, Judith could not help the momentary bitterness which swept through her. Were *all* men sexually treacherous?

But then she saw the way Raymond and Joyce were looking at each other and simply could not harbour resentment in her heart. They were a well-suited couple, a much better match than herself and Raymond. Not only that, but Raymond's revelation meant she hadn't shattered his life with her own behaviour. She was free of guilt. *Free!*

The enormity of her relief sent her eyes flying to Alex, who'd been watching her with a degree of concerned speculation. Her joyous response to Raymond's announcement was mirrored in the instant brightening of his whole face and she realised that what he'd told her earlier was true.

Everything he'd done that day was for her—to win her love. Why else would he still be here? If all he'd wanted was to finish what they'd started that night seven years ago, he'd have packed up and flown home by now. Yes, he'd acted boldly this morning in making love to her, but not out of wickedness. Out of desperation. And love.

He loved her. She could see it in his eyes.

Her tender smile was enough to make his handsome face break into the broadest grin. He hurried forward to curl an arm around her waist and pull her to his side.

Judith went without a single qualm, for she knew this was where she was meant to be. By Alex's side, for better for worse, from this day forward, till death them did part. Their love had lasted a long time with little to feed it. Now that they had found each other again, it would grow stronger and stronger with each passing day.

'My God, I'm surrounded by adulterers!' Margaret exclaimed. 'I'm not going to stay and be a party to this! Mario, take me home!'

'Yes, Mario,' Raymond said scathingly. 'Do something useful for once and take the silly cow home.'

Margaret looked as if she was about to have apoplexy. She opened her mouth to say something, then shut it again, speechless in her fury. She flounced over to the Jaguar where she waited, tight-lipped, at the passenger door for a sighing Mario to do the honours.

'How did all this come about?' Judith whispered in Alex's ear while Margaret and Mario made their exit. 'Who told Raymond about us? You?'

'In a roundabout way,' he whispered back. 'Raymond rang from Joyce's barely a minute after you left. When I told him you were on your way over there, he thought you must have found out about them. Thinking he was talking to a fellow man of the world, he made some very interesting admissions to me. Not only has he been carrying on with Joyce behind your back, but it seems he's made her pregnant. Apparently, she rang to tell him so last night. He told you some cock-and-bull story and hotfooted it over to Joyce's this morning with God knows what in mind.

'Once he got used to the news, however, he suddenly realised just how much Joyce meant to him and that it should be her he was marrying, not you. To be brutally frank, I think he was only marrying you because he thought Joyce was too old to have a baby. You are young and beautiful and would have provided him with a healthy, handsome child.

'The thought of having a beautiful young wife on his arm did things for his ego as well. Raymond has an ego a mile wide. I have no doubt that he never had any intention of terminating his sexual relationship with Joyce. He thought he could have the best of both worlds.'

Judith was sceptical of this till she recalled what Raymond had said the previous night about not being able to have it all. 'I think you're right, Alex,' she murmured.

'He actually tried to justify himself over the phone by saying that someone as young and lovely as you would have no trouble finding someone else to marry, whereupon I told him how right he was and that that someone was me! When I told him what had happened seven years ago and again this weekend, he seemed more relieved than annoyed. He also didn't seem too worried when I expressed concern that you obviously hadn't gone to Joyce's and that you'd run away because you were ashamed of betraying his supposed love. As I said before, a sensitive fellow, your Raymond.'

'Be kind, Alex. We've found each other again, haven't we? We can afford to be generous.'

'I wanted to smash his teeth in when he first told me about Joyce. How could any man do that to you? But then I realised he didn't love you one iota and I instantly recovered. I also realised that *you* might be having *my* baby and suddenly nothing else seemed important. Have you thought of that, my darling? That we might have made a son or a daughter this morning?'

Actually, she hadn't. But now that she did it was the most wonderful thought. She lifted loving eyes to his and murmured, 'I certainly hope so.'

It was the right thing to say. The happiness on Alex's face shone like a thousand stars and his arm tightened around her. 'God, I love you,' he said. 'I've always loved you.'

He kissed her upturned lips and Judith's heart filled with joy. All the lonely years melted away and she knew that at last she was going to be happy. Not lukewarm happy but brightly, burstingly happy.

And she was going to have babies. Lots of babies. Alex's babies.

'Ahem!'

They broke apart to find themselves standing on the pavement with only Raymond and Joyce.

'Mario and Margaret have gone,' Raymond announced drily.

'Poor Margaret,' Joyce murmured sympathetically. 'She's not very happy with Mario, you know.'

'I know. But she's made her bed, Joyce. She'll just have to lie in it. Don't you worry your dear sweet head about it. We're all happy in our beds, aren't we?'

His comment didn't seem to please Joyce and Judith suddenly realised what the problem might be.

'Raymond did tell you, didn't he, Joyce?' she began carefully.

'Tell me what?'

'That *we've* never shared a bed. Never. Not once.'

'Yes, he did, but...um...'

But she hadn't really believed him. Judith sighed her acceptance of the situation. Raymond only had himself to blame, she supposed. He probably deserved Joyce's scepticism. Still, Judith did so want Raymond and Joyce to be happy, even if they couldn't be as brilliantly happy as she and Alex were going to be.

She reached out and placed a reassuring hand on Joyce's arm. 'Raymond and I were friends, not lovers,' she told the doubting woman. 'You are both to him. A friend *and* a lover. I have never meant to Raymond what you mean to him. Alex tells me you're going to have a baby.'

'Yes. In the new year.'

'How lovely. I hope you'll be very happy. You deserve it. And you too, Raymond, though I'm not sure you deserve it quite so much. You should have told me you were in love with Joyce.'

Raymond looked a little put out by the criticism. 'And you should have told me you were in love with Alex,' he countered, 'instead of letting me think you disliked him.'

'I didn't realise I *was* in love with him.'

'Which, I think, covers the situation between myself and Joyce,' Raymond defended. 'But we're all sure now, aren't we? I think a bottle of champagne is called for, don't you?'

'Expectant mothers shouldn't drink, Raymond,' Joyce reminded him sweetly on the way into the house.

'In that case, only soft drink for you, my love.'

'Perhaps I should only have soft drink too, just in case,' Judith joined in, bringing a startled glance from Raymond. He began shaking his head.

'Alex said I didn't know you, Judith. I can see he was right. But I must ask you a couple of questions to satisfy my curiosity. Were you really on your way to the airport when you left here, and not to Joyce's, as you told him? Alex was insisting I drive him to the airport in pursuit of you when you turned up.'

'Yes, I was going to the airport,' she confessed, then glanced up at Alex. 'Yes, I was running away again, Alex. I admit it.'

He bent to kiss her on her nose. 'But you came back. And *how*. I'm so proud of you.'

'I'm pretty proud of myself.'

Raymond looked disgruntled at this exchange. 'Well, all right, I'll give you that one, Alex, but what exactly have you got in that red suitcase Alex is carrying?'

'What? Oh...er...just clothes and things,' Judith

said evasively. No way could she ever explain that the only things she'd taken with her were her multitude of furry friends, her toilet bag and some underclothes. She'd been going to send for some more clothes later, via Mrs Cobb.

'See, Alex?' Raymond jeered pompously. 'It's not full of silly toys. You were wrong. You don't know Judith that well after all.'

Alex smiled down at Judith, who tried not to look too surprised or guilty. How had Alex known? And then she remembered waking up yesterday and finding her bedroom door open. He'd come and seen and understood, as no one had understood before, except perhaps her poor down-trodden father.

'Could be, Raymond,' he returned magnanimously, showing Judith that he didn't need to score points over another male to feel good about himself. She sighed her pleasure at this reassuring sign of adult maturity, then winked at him in confession and complicity over what was in fact stuffed into that suitcase.

'Peter Panda would be proud of you,' she whispered as they followed Raymond and Joyce inside.

Alex's expression was wry. 'I suppose I'm going to have to share a bed with Peter Panda, aren't I?' he whispered back.

'I'm afraid so.'

'Oh, well…I've had more formidable foes. But if you start talking to him while I'm making love to you he goes!'

'If I start talking to him while you're making love to me,' she retorted, 'then it'll be *you* who'll go!'

Their eyes met and they burst out laughing.

EPILOGUE

THE helicopter came abruptly over the crest of the range and Judith gasped at the view. Below lay the cutest cove with the cutest little township nestled against its shores. Only one pier jutted out into the gentle blue waters, with a small selection of fishing and pleasure craft moored on either side.

She would have said something to Alex but his headphones and the roaring noise rather precluded easy conversation, unless one wanted to yell. The helicopter swooped down over the bay and the town, giving her a closer view of the prettiest place she had ever seen. It banked, then soared back up the face of the steep, tree-covered hills which hugged the town in a U-shape. Everything was a deep green, the vegetation dense and lush.

A clearing came into view at the top into which Alex masterfully angled then landed the highly manoeuvrable craft. They'd been in the air for less than an hour since leaving the heliport in Sydney.

The wind outside was brisk and fresh but they had dressed for it. Alex had said he wanted to show her something special that morning, but had refused to elaborate. It was a week after all had been revealed and they had just surfaced from the hotel room where Alex had taken Judith from Raymond's place.

It had taken Alex that long, he'd claimed, to be convinced that she really loved him. Judith thought she'd done a pretty good job of convincing him.

'Oh, Alex, what a magnificent place!' she exclaimed now, walking to the edge of the clearing and looking out at the ocean then down at the tiny township. 'Do you own it?'

'Yep. Every single acre in these hills. What do you think?'

'I think it *is* very special, like you said.'

'I'm going to build a resort here—and before you say anything it's not going to be one of those ghastly over-commercialised places. It's going to be an environmentally friendly establishment, totally solar-powered, with individual log cabins for guests and buildings which blend right into the surroundings. The sewerage system will be a unique new treatment which makes it clean enough to be used for watering lawns and gardens. Nothing will be pumped out into the ocean.'

'What do the locals think?'

'They're all for it. The fishing industry which used to support the town went into a slump years ago and all the young people are leaving to go to the city to find work. I'm also going to buy several pleasure craft for tourist fishing trips, coastal cruises and the best draw-card of all—whale-watching. I've already lined up some of the unemployed fishermen to man the boats and they think I'm the ant's pants.'

Judith put her arms around his waist and hugged him close. 'I think you're the ant's pants too.'

'I haven't finished yet. You might change your mind in a minute.'

She pulled back, wary now. 'Tell me the whole awful truth.'

His face was serious. 'I want to live here and raise my family here, Judith. Look, I know you're a city girl but I'm sick and tired of the fast life. And I'm heartily sick of living in Greg's various penthouses around Australia. Talk about glass houses! I want some peace and quiet and simplicity. If you say yes, I'll build us a house right here. A good solid Aussie home with a nice pitched roof and cool wide verandahs all around.'

'Right here?' She pointed down at the spot she was standing on.

'Yes. Right there.'

Judith's heart filled with happiness. 'I...er...I think I might be able to suffer that,' she choked out.

'You would?'

'Oh, Alex, I'd love it! All I've ever wanted is a simple and peaceful life. And this place...this is heaven!'

'Yes, but what about your nursing? I know it means a lot to you—or it used to. Or don't you want to do that any longer?'

'I do, but I think having babies will fully occupy me for a while. Anyway, if you build a resort here, then there'll always be work for me as a nurse around here if I want it. As long as you don't mind my going back to work, that is.'

'Whatever makes you happy makes me happy.'

She smiled her satisfaction with the man she loved. Underneath that cynical façade he'd worn for a while he was just the same as the man she'd first met: sweet and kind, deep-thinking and caring.

He'd obviously been terribly hurt by what Simon had done to his sister, and even more hurt at having let Simon—charming liar that he was—convince him that it had not been his fault. Alex had even been going to let him marry *her*, he had confessed, till he'd seen his two-faced friend with that married woman on the night of the party. Judith could well understand how shocked Alex had been when he'd thought she knew about that. She shuddered to think how close she had come to losing him over that ghastly misunderstanding.

Which reminded her…

'Alex?'

'Yes?'

'You know how you said you were going to take me down to meet your family next week…?'

'Yes?'

'I…er…I think there's something you should know—and please, please don't be mad at Karen.'

'Mad at Karen? About what?'

She told him then, about his sister's visit, and about what she had thought.

'Oh, God,' was all he said before hugging her close. Neither of them spoke for ages.

'You don't believe that any more, do you?' he finally asked painfully. 'You don't think I did what I did that night out of revenge, do you?'

'No. Not at all.'

'Thank God.'

'Don't say anything to her, Alex. Let her think we've just met again and fallen in love. Don't ever let her know we were in love back then. She'd be so upset.'

He pulled back to stare down at her. 'So generous,' he murmured. 'Not a word from you in all this time. Yet you could have defended yourself with this. Why didn't you?'

'I thought about it. But it never seemed the right moment. You were pretty damning in your preconceptions of me, Alex. I didn't think it would make any difference.'

He groaned. 'I hate to say it, but you're probably right. I was crazy with hurt at having found you after all that time, but belonging to someone else. I grasped at straws and believed anything that blackened your character so that I wouldn't fall under your spell again. I feel so guilty about that, my darling. It never ceases to amaze me that you forgave me.'

'There were excuses for both of us, Alex. Besides, the past is over now, isn't it? We did find each other again and we're going to be happy together.'

He clasped her close, then kissed her.

Oh, yes, they were going to be very happy, Judith decided. She was going to make sure of that. Fate had given her a second chance at love and she was going to grasp it with both hands. She would never run away from life, or passion, ever again. She would embrace it, cherish it, treasure it.

Life with Alex might not always be smooth. What

marriage was? But they would make it together. Of that she was certain. For they had one very important thing going for them: the strength and staying power of true love.

Two months later they were married. Nine months afterwards they moved into their home with their baby son, Vincent. Eighteen months later stage one of the resort opened, with Judith already pregnant again. The town wanted Alex to run for council. He said he would, if Judith agreed. She did.

Take 2 bestselling love stories FREE

Plus get a FREE surprise gift!

HARLEQUIN PRESENTS®

Everyone has special occasions in their life—an engagement, a wedding, an anniversary...or maybe the birth of a baby.

These are times of celebration and excitement, and we're delighted to bring you a special new series called...

One special occasion—that changes your life forever!

Celebrate *The Big Event!* with great books by some of your favorite authors:

September 1998—BRIDE FOR A YEAR
by Kathryn Ross (#1981)
October 1998—MARRIAGE MAKE UP
by Penny Jordan (#1983)
November 1998—RUNAWAY FIANCÉE
by Sally Wentworth (#1992)
December 1998—BABY INCLUDED!
by Mary Lyons (#1997)

Look in the back pages of any *Big Event* book to find out how to receive a set of sparkling wineglasses.

Available wherever Harlequin books are sold.

HARLEQUIN®
Makes any time special ™

Toast the special events in your life with Harlequin Presents®!

With the purchase of *two* Harlequin Presents® BIG EVENT books, you can send in for two sparkling plum-colored Wineglasses. A retail value of $19.95!

ACT NOW TO COLLECT TWO BEAUTIFUL WINEGLASSES!

On the official proof-of-purchase coupon below, fill in your name, address and zip or postal code and send it, plus $2.99 U.S./$3.99 CAN. for postage and handling (check or money order—please do not send cash) payable to Harlequin Books, to: In the U.S.: 3010 Walden Avenue, P.O. Box 9077, Buffalo, N.Y. 14269-9077; In Canada: P.O. Box 609, Fort Erie, Ontario L2A 5X3. Please allow 4-6 weeks for delivery. Order your set of wineglasses now! Quantities are limited. Offer for the Plum Wineglasses expires December 31, 1998.

Harlequin Presents®—The Big Event!

OFFICIAL PROOF OF PURCHASE

"Please send me my TWO Wineglasses"

Name. _____

Address: _____

City: _____

State/Prov.: _____ Zip/Postal Code: _____

Account Number: _____ **097 KGS CSA6 193-3**

HPBEPOP

HARLEQUIN®
Makes any time special ™

The Gifts of Christmas

Join three of your favorite historical romance
authors as they celebrate the festive season
in their own special style!

Mary Balogh
Merline Lovelace &
Suzanne Barclay

bring you a captivating collection
of historical romances.

Indulge in the seasonal delights of Regency and
medieval England and share in the discovery of
unforgettable love with *The Gifts of Christmas*.

Available in November 1998,
at your favorite retail store.

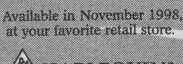

For a limited time, Harlequin and Silhouette have an offer you just can't refuse.

In November and December 1998:

BUY **ANY** TWO HARLEQUIN
OR SILHOUETTE BOOKS and
SAVE $10.00
off future purchases

OR BUY ANY THREE HARLEQUIN OR SILHOUETTE BOOKS
AND **SAVE $20.00** OFF FUTURE PURCHASES!

(each coupon is good for $1.00 off the purchase of two
Harlequin or Silhouette books)

....

JUST BUY 2 HARLEQUIN OR SILHOUETTE BOOKS, SEND US YOUR
NAME, ADDRESS AND 2 PROOFS OF PURCHASE (CASH REGISTER
RECEIPTS) AND HARLEQUIN WILL SEND YOU A COUPON BOOKLET
WORTH **$10.00 OFF** FUTURE PURCHASES OF HARLEQUIN OR
SILHOUETTE BOOKS IN 1999. SEND US 3 PROOFS OF PURCHASE AND
WE WILL SEND YOU 2 COUPON BOOKLETS WITH A TOTAL SAVING OF
$20.00. (ALLOW 4-6 WEEKS DELIVERY) OFFER EXPIRES
DECEMBER 31, 1998.

....

I accept your offer! Please send me a coupon booklet(s), to:

NAME: _____

ADDRESS: _____

CITY: _____ STATE/PROV.: _____ POSTAL/ZIP CODE: _____

Send your name and address, along with your cash register
receipts for proofs of purchase, to:

In the U.S.	In Canada
Harlequin Books	Harlequin Books
P.O. Box 9057	P.O. Box 622
Buffalo, NY	Fort Erie, Ontario
14269	L2A 5X3

Coming Next Month

HARLEQUIN PRESENTS®

THE BEST HAS JUST GOTTEN BETTER!

#1995 MARRIED BY CHRISTMAS Carole Mortimer
Lilii was mortified when she woke up in Patrick Devlin's bed! He wasn't about to let her forget it, either. Patrick would save her father's chain of hotels...if she married him—by Christmas!

#1996 THE BRIDAL BED Helen Bianchin
(Do Not Disturb)
For her mother's wedding, Suzanne and her ex-fiancé, Sloan, had to play the part of a happy, soon-to-marry couple! After sharing a room—and a bed!—their pretend passion became real...and another wedding was on the agenda!

#1997 BABY INCLUDED! Mary Lyons
(The Big Event!)
Lord Ratcliffe was delighted that Eloise had turned up at his surprise birthday party. He'd always thought she was an ordinary American tourist; but in fact she was an international sex symbol...and secretly carrying his baby!

#1998 A HUSBAND'S PRICE Diana Hamilton
Six years ago when Adam and Claudia had split up, he'd left a part of himself with her—a child. Now Adam's help comes with a hefty price tag—that Claudia become his wife. Faced with bankruptcy and a custody battle, Claudia has no choice....

#1999 A NANNY FOR CHRISTMAS Sara Craven
(Nanny Wanted!)
Dominic Ashton thought Phoebe was a wonderful stand-in mom for little Tara; it was a pity she couldn't stay longer. But Phoebe had her reasons for going: if Dominic had forgotten their first meeting years before, she certainly hadn't!

#2000 MORGAN'S CHILD Anne Mather
(Harlequin Presents' 2000th title!)
Four years after the death of her husband in war-torn Africa, Felicity Riker at last had a new man...a new life. Then she heard that Morgan had been found *alive*...and that he was on his was back to reclaim his long-lost wife....